Strangled
Twisted Tales of Familiar Faces
Stephen Wertzbaugher

M4L Publishing

Vitriol

THE INSIDE OF MY skull burns with liquid fire. Taloned fingers tear open the surface to my soul, peel back the leprous darkness, pour scalding acid into the ragged crevices. I am an onion, my layers black with rot and decay.

Shimmering eyes, not my own, peer out from the shadows of my mind, dripping ravenous anticipation. A diseased tongue darts from between putrescent lips to taste the soul quivering beneath the prison of my glorious curse.

Roiling vines of crimson-stained golden red hair sprout from my shaved and scarred scalp. They seethe and writhe through the air, bullwhip-tipped ends flaying open the bared flesh of the naked priest I straddle, fouling the wounds with demonic, paralyzing venom. He jerks with each exquisite kiss, his tormented shrieks muffled by thick, winding strands of hair gagging his mouth.

A chorus of psychotic voices whisper through my unraveling thoughts, their jabbering music scraping the sanity from my consciousness.

I close my eyes, clench my fists against the rising cacophony, and beat the sides of my head as the unraveling ends of my mind twist into a tangled knot. "Not yet," I whisper. "Not yet."

The voices quiet for a heartbeat, sulk back into the deeper darkness, clinging to my corrupted soul. I sigh, open my eyes and smile, welcoming the breath of peace I have been allowed to enjoy.

Augustus Matthews, the Confessor of the Damned, who aided in the murder of my beloved Eric, quivers beneath me.

My smile broadens into a maddened grin.

"Vitriol."

I slide my gaze upward, past the priest's face, blow out a slow, dreamy sigh as I stare at the *Nativity with St. Francis and St. Lawrence* by Caravaggio hanging above the bed. Demented light and shadows tossed from the television on the other side of the bedroom glint off the canvas, fluttering through the brush strokes and images. The muffled sounds of exaggerated moans and smutty squeals worm through the stale air, leer over my bare shoulders.

I lean my forearms on the man's hairy, pot-bellied pig stomach, the bristly ends of the curly hairs scratching my skin. Giggling from their caress, I close my eyes, dreaming of feathers and the melodic trickle of water meandering over the silty bottom of a sleepy brook. I wriggle my thighs suggestively where they straddle the priest's paunchy hips.

Candlelight quivers around us, the amorous aromas of musk, vetiver, and floral jasmine embracing us, brushing our flesh and bones with lustful kisses.

"It is an eloquent word," I say.

I smile coyly. "One that rolls off the tip of the tongue, does it not? Breathes into it a certain *Je ne sais quoi*." I swivel my hand through the smoky air in an elaborate gesture, reach over to stroke his cheek with the back of my fingers, sliming the sweat clinging to his pasty face.

He trembles beneath my touch, his eyes wide, the light brown irises swallowed whole by his dilated pupils. Sweat glistens from his brow, rainbow-colored globules dribbling down his temples, plopping into the bedding, and soaking the silk, the salty sea spreading sluggishly through the crumpled fabric.

A mumbled agreement creeps from the edges of the knotted strands of hair spanning his puffy lips.

My sanity slips another stripped gear.

I clap my hands in giddy excitement. "I knew you would agree. I just knew it!" I squint into the shadows clinging to the paneled ceiling, watch the flickering candlelight snake through the darkness as I bite my lower lip. "Vitriol," I whisper wistfully. "It is an appropriate word, I think. One deep with buried meaning and purpose." I knead his stomach with my fingers, digging my nails into his skin, and drawing shallow, crimson furrows down the mound of quivering flesh.

The tangled forest of my hair continues to bloom, blotting out the flickering candlelight.

He whimpers, his heart sputtering for an instant, rancid breath leaking from beneath the edges of the braided tangles, gluing his mouth closed. I wrinkle my nose in disgust. "Vitriol," I breathe, looking down.

Furrowing my brow, I pout my lip in mock concern as I gaze into his terrified eyes. "Please forgive me, Father," I say, leaning forward to stroke his cheek. "I am so very, very sorry, my dearest. Truly, I am. I did not think."

I yank the hair from his mouth, crush it into a ball in my fist. "This was to be our special night. And here I am, blathering on like a love-struck schoolgirl, my thoughts traipsing aimlessly through the wilderness."

I touch my fingers to my lips, lean up and over his paunch, press them to his quivering mouth. "Please accept my deepest and sincerest apologies. I shall endeavor for the rest of our brief time together this evening to focus the whole of my amorous attentions to bringing you the same pleasures you seek from the activities beyond." I glance over my shoulder at the television hanging on the opposite wall. A man and two women engage in carnal activities that ten years ago would have made me blush to watch.

No longer.

I flinch a mirthless smirk, push a creased and crinkled ten-year-old photo of myself and my beloved Eric arm-in-arm, our eyes drinking in the essence of each other. "Do you remember my dearly loved Eric?" I ask.

His eyes widen. Small, whimpering sounds slither from his quivering mouth.

I lay the photo upon his stomach, push a second crumpled and crinkled photo of a prenatal ultrasound at his face. Two identical fetuses seem to hug each other within the comforting confines of a womb. My womb.

"I shall offer you a small mercy if you can tell me what this is. And who it is." I smile, though I feel no humor.

A barely audible cry snakes from between his limp lips. A tear wells, rolls from his eye.

I lay the photo beside the other on his stomach and sulk."No?" I ask. "Nothing? Nothing at all?"

I feel him quiver beneath me and wriggle my thighs in response ."Perhaps we should concentrate on other, more carnal activities to engage your memories."

I pause and wink. "I hope that when our time together is at an end, you will continue to think of me as fondly as I of you." I slide from his hips, bare feet thumping against the carpeted floor.

Sighing, spinning in lazy circles, I giggle with delight and hug my chest as I dig my toes into the squishy feel of the Berber, the way it titillates my skin, luxuriating in its tender and welcoming embrace. I pause before the television, cock my head to the side, watching the naked bodies as they slither and snake against each other, the animalistic grunting, the contrived and theatrical moans and groans of illusory pleasure.

A frown creases my brow, bile creeping into my throat, disgust clenching at my thoughts. I swallow it down, embracing the loathing crouching in my mind as an enraptured smile crosses my slender lips. I look back over my shoulder. "Such...sensuality, my darling. Such...love. Such...devotion. I do not understand how one could not become enraptured by...such wondrous couplings."

A hesitation, my rhyme tingling the tip of my tongue, teasing my mouth. The ends of my hair writhe with impatience and enthusiasm, the golden-red strands squirming as they worm from my scalp. Flaming torment skins the back of my skull. The voices rise, their deranged chorus stabbing my crumbling sanity.

"Not yet," I whisper. "I am not yet ready."

The maelstrom quiets once more, impatient, a rabid dog straining against its chain. The demons will not wait much longer.

I lick the verses away, clench my jaw, scraping the words from my lips with my teeth, tasting the tangy bitterness of blood upon my chin.

My hair flutters for an instant. The wispy tendrils fall limp against my bare shoulders, the tangled strands a few inches longer than a heartbeat before, but not yet an unruly and twisted briar patch choking with brambles. I breathe a sigh, draw myself up, a greasy chuckle dribbling from my lips. I turn. "Shall I turn the volume up?" I ask. "So that you may enjoy this lustful fornication all the more?" I brandish the television remote.

Gasping shrieks stutter from the man where he lies, paralyzed, his fleshy, roly-poly limbs vibrating the bed. Seas of sweat soak the sheets surrounding him, the salty stench curdling the euphoric scents wafting from the burning candles scattered throughout the bedroom.

I twitch a disgusted smile, skim my gaze over the gold and silver crucifix nailed above the door frame. Ironic? Perhaps. How many times has this priest crucified his lord and savior while committing his vile and reprehensible acts against innocent flesh?

I clench my fists, muscles twisting and knotting, body trembling as I turn my eyes to the clustered images of the Nativity where they lean over a stout oak writing desk, watchful, innocent and childlike, the expression from the Mother Mary serene and content.

Did she know the monster that lay on the bed in this room? Did she suspect his nature or the true character that hid behind the carefully constructed mask, maintained with careful diligence throughout the years? The disarming smile. The gentle touch and kind, inviting words? Until the fiend lurking within could no longer wait, its lustful appetite demanding release and sustenance.

But if the Blessed Mary were truly the mother of God, would she not know? How could she not? Or at least suspect? Perhaps she did and chose not to notice or to look the other way, hiding her knowledge behind a thinly veiled and tattered cloak of self-righteous superiority.

What was the verse? An image came. My Oma's opened Bible. Shriveled fingers caressing the red ink bleeding across and down the page, the paper thin and fragile, easily torn and broken like the wing of a newly hatched bird. Peter's question, "How many times do I forgive?" Jesus's response.

I crush the memory, grind it into the dirt beside my charred and blackened forgiveness, the numbers torn limb from limb by the ravening wolves masquerading as sheep. Seventy times seven didn't begin to cover his sins. Seventy million times seven didn't scratch the blazing surface of his iniquities.

Too much time come and gone. Too many chances lost; innocent souls annihilated because of the Virgin's hopeful inaction and faithful reliance on a God that did not seem to care.

My lover and soulmate murdered by Mother Gothel, a woman I trusted to save my soul, and tossed from the open window of his tower chamber by this...man of God.

My children stolen from my womb by the same woman.

My family lost. Perhaps forever.

I wouldn't look the other way. I wouldn't rely on justice from an apathetic and indefensible system that ignored the corruption gnawing away at the crumbling cornerstone supporting its rotting foundations. I could not. Not now. Not ever. Mother Gothel had taken everything from me. And now, I would take everything and more from her.

I slap a sultry smirk across my face, stroll seductively toward the foot of the bed, dancing my fingers up a shaggy leg, stopping at the top of the inside of his thigh.

I stare critically for a breath. "My love," I say in astonishment. "I have been away from you for too long, it seems." I climb onto the bed, straddle his hips, bury the repugnance bubbling beneath my expression. "But alas, my love. Time slips past, whether we will it so or not, and I must no longer tarry."

I lean my elbows on his paunch. "You do understand, do you not...Father Confessor?"

I snigger, toy absently with a clammy mound of corkscrew curly chest hair as I lean over him and glare into his panic-round eyes. "Do you still not yet recognize me or my children?" I allow the disappointment to skip across my face. "Perhaps I should not be surprised. It has been ten years and three months since you tossed my beloved Eric from his tower chamber window. Ten years of grief and rage for me. Ten years of rusting memory for you."

Another coy smile. I wink at him. "How many others have you massacred in the name of God since I have been gone?"

Hopeless recognition flashes behind his eyes, dragged through the gluttonous muck by terror. His mouth trembles, bloated lips straining. "Rosalinde," he whispers. "You were to be the salvation of our world." His face twists agony and abhorrence. "Instead, you—"

"What?" I snap. I lean forward, eagerness gleaming in my eyes, my lips parted with expectation. "You thought I was dead? That I would not come back to avenge that which was stolen from me?" I suck in a ragged breath, blind rage scorching away the last of my reticence.

"You promised me paradise and a new beginning, one not soiled by the curse borne by my family for generations! You swore to purge me of the demons nesting in the core of my soul! Instead, you took everything from me and left me to die, one day at a time, as grief gnawed away my sanity!"

He shoves out an exhausted breath; the tension clenching his body melting into grimy puddles.

I trace the ragged line of the knife scar running down his cheek, a reminder of the gash I gave him the night he and Mother Gothel murdered my Eric. "Bless me, Father, for you have greatly sinned. It has been never since your last confession and now it is too late for your redemption."

His head quivers. "You should not have come back."

Rage grinds the few remaining pebbles of my grief into dust.

The clock on his desk chimes three.

Calm hugs my tormented soul in its silky embrace.

"It is time for me to go, my love. To leave you with your dreams of what might have been but should never have occurred." I sit back, place a single stem of Rapunzel upon his chest, the delicate violet petals fluttering to the beat of his tremulous breathing. "A small token of my enmity."

I wink, plant my palms upon his paunch, allow the whispers to crawl from their shadows as I recite the verses of my song:

Rapunzel!

Rapunzel!

Let down your hair!

Then I may claim your golden stair!

The words spill from between my parted lips, the sweet siren tones of the voices within me wrapping the shivering air with their delicate, sensual embrace.

I bite through the inside of my cheek as twisting agony knots my gut, snarls and tangles my muscles, contorting my body into a collapsing star. Its light and life sucked from the universe of my mind.

I stab my nails through his skin, piercing flesh and fat, focusing on the steaming warmth kissing my fingertips, my thoughts burning to ash, utterly consumed by a storm of fiery hail.

He bucks beneath me, an agonized scream ripping from his throat.

My hair writhes and wriggles, the golden red strands elongating, twirling and twisting together as they stretch and lengthen, the individual tendrils wrapping into plaits and braids, thickening, growing stouter, root and limb-like. My hair snakes and slithers along his body, creeps and crawls, hooking dagger-sharp spikes into his open mouth and ears, weaving crowns of thorns about his eyes.

I pant, heart thudding, twisting and warping, staring down at him.

His eyes, blood welling from their corners, beg forgiveness.

I shake my head, lick the scarlet from my mouth. "Too late," I say. "Too late."

The ends of my hair plunge into his mouth, tunnel through his ears, gouge out his eyes.

I shriek.

Grimm-Locked

Detective Locke

Detective William Locke stands at the foot of his wife Olivia's grave. Ten years of weather grime coats the rough-hewn granite surface, obscuring the name and dates chiseled into the stone. He wipes away the tears staining his stubbled cheeks, snuffs up the watery snot dripping from his nose, and shudders a grief-ridden sigh. His gaze wanders to the two smaller graves embracing hers. Their son, Jacob, three, and their daughter, Deborah, five.

Both drowned by Olivia in their bathtub, before she shaved her head with a straight razor and killed herself with his gun.

The last of the night's yawning shadows slink back before the rising sun, dragging his ragged silhouette with them, leaving behind the lusterless slate gray stone marking the head of Olivia's grave. Her name and the dates of her birth and death glare back at him, mocking the grief twisting his gut into knots. Beneath the dates hunkers uncarved oblivion, a testament to his obdurate rage over her unforgivable acts.

The newly shorn dew-blanketed grass carpeting the graves of his family glitters in the blossoming morning light like an infinite universe of exploding stars. An ambivalent breeze ruffles his salt-and-pepper hair, slides down to scratch his two-day old beard, the black shot through with strands of gray.

Ten years. And still buried in grief and rage. Why? Because she never trusted him with her secret.

"Why didn't you trust me?"

He clutches a shabby and tattered copy of *The Original Folk and Fairy Tales of the Brothers Grimm* in a trembling hand. The gilded lettering on the front cover and spine chafed and eroded to a dirty reflection of the original. The head of a creased and crumpled bookmark thrusts itself from the yellowed pages, trumpeting the location of the folktale, *Rapunzel*, Olivia's obsession. The story that drove her to murder their children and then kill herself ten years ago.

His obsession now.

A crow caws, the raucous screech stabbing him between his shoulder blades.

Locke tears his gaze from the graves and scowls at the bird, it's pitch-black outline smirching the flowering sunlight.

An answering croak from the other side of the dirt-packed trail hammers the air.

Locke cringes, gritting his teeth as he drags his eyes back to Olivia's grave.

The air shudders.

You came.

"I almost didn't," Locke says.

I'm glad you did. I've been lonely.

Locke purses his lips and shifts his feet. "Jacob and Deborah?"

An indecisive pause.

The air dancing around him chills. Locke's breath boils steam, the roiling clouds swirling upward into extinction. He pulls his rumpled suit coat tighter across his chest. "Where are they?"

They refuse to come to me anymore. They are still angry.

Locke snorts.

I love you.

He shivers. Rage explodes. He brandishes the book at Olivia's headstone. "Why?" he shouts. "Why did you kill them?"

Silence. The scrape of shifting certainty against his mind. *I couldn't let my family's curse take them like it had taken me. I had to end it.*

His fury clutches his chest for another heartbeat before skulking back into the abyss of his anguish and torment. "You could have told me," he says. "I could have helped you...and them."

A bitter laugh.

Locke cringes.

Would you have believed me?

Hesitation.

The word forms on his lips.

Memories of their life together flash through his thoughts. Olivia, her silver blonde hair shimmering gold in the early morning and late afternoon light. Worn in a short pixie cut, the brambly ends always peeking shyly from her scalp. Her obsessive insistence that she keep her hair shorn. The ensuing arguments when he pressed the issue, his desire to see her hair grown long. Something for him to admire, run his fingers through. A place for him to bury himself after they made love.

Darkness mutes the light glinting through his remembrances. Olivia's sudden and unexpected moodiness when her hair began to grow out, the storm clouds incessantly hovering in her mind. The way her demeanor changed on a dime, often leaving him perplexed and confused.

Knowing now what he didn't know then, it all made sense. But he didn't know. She never told him. And if he had known?

The word huddling on his parted lips dies in fiery awareness. The ashes fall, scattering in the fitful breeze. "No," he says. "I would not have believed you."

A sigh caresses his cheek.

Locke drops the book. He closes his eyes, presses his fingers into the caress, hoping to catch her touch before it evaporates.

He stifles a sob, pounds the top of Olivia's headstone. "You didn't have to kill our children."

She discovered my secret. I couldn't allow her to take our children.

"Who?"

Mother—

Locke's phone rings, startling him.

When did he fall to his knees?

Fetid breath washes over him. He gags, unsteady breath grasping at the breeze, his hands clawing at emptiness.

"Don't go," he cries. "Please!"

Nothingness answers him.

His phone continues to ring.

Locke presses his forehead against Olivia's headstone. He stifles a sob, shoves the anger down into the muck sloughing his soul.

He answers his phone.

It's Keith Fox, his partner. "We've got a body. Saint Thomas Aquinas parish. It's bad."

Locke remains silent. The cold seeping from the chiseled marble embraces his flesh, inviting him to give up and join Olivia in blessed oblivion.

"Locke? Are you there? Did you hear me?"

His partner's uneasy tone shakes the lethargy from his stumbling thoughts.

"Yeah," Locke says. "Saint Thomas Aquinas parish. Be there in fifteen."

The Mourning After

I SIT UPON A sanded and burnished park bench, the wooden slats pressing into the back of my legs. I watch the sun creep above a mountain-ragged horizon, the biting taste of blood-smeared memory eating holes through my thoughts. Has it only been a few hours since the demons and the curse I harbor feasted on the soul of Augustus Matthews and made him pay for his sins?

The irony of his fate does not escape me. The Confessor of the Damned. A priest of the Heralds of the Seventh Seal responsible for giving last rights to lost souls afflicted by irreversible demon possession before their expurgation through fire. A purification no one survived.

I had become Augustus Matthews' Confessor of the Damned.

Dust-tinged sunlight slants through a rotting plum and banana-colored sky. Robin chicks' raucous demands for breakfast echo through the shivering air. They bellyache from the clutching confines of their camouflaged nests, anchored within the leafy heights of ash and maples marching mindlessly across the rolling park landscape. The pungent odors of roses and lilacs stagger drunkenly together along the winding gravel paths; hand in hand, heads leaning in, faces touching, to share their deepest and darkest secrets between slobbering kisses.

A breath of fresh air pushes through the bushy tangles hanging down from above. The deep green foliage titters, its half-whispered snickers tapping me on the back of my head, the unending prick of tiny, invisible fingers scattering my unsettled thoughts, causing my skull to throb.

Tap. Tap. Tap. Tap.

I lean back on the park bench. Splintering wood pokes the backs of my thighs through my pink floral chiffon dress, calves splayed apart, knees pressed together, mud-painted bare feet digging into the dewy grass. A lonely, silver satin stiletto-heeled sandal hunkers on the seat beside me, the ankle strap twitching to the thrumming beat of my heart. My trembling hands crush my hat in my lap. The hem of my dress flutters against my shins, tickling silken smooth skin. A few errant crimson splatters paint the skirt.

I rub at a splotch, smearing the scarlet deeper into the gossamer strands. Ruined. How could I have been so careless? I should have undressed myself instead of allowing that pig to claw the dress from my body like a ravening baboon. I shudder, wipe my hands on the skirt, rub them down my arms, attempting to scrub off the screaming meemies dancing a chorus line up and down my body.

Why did you wear the dress in the first place if you knew he would sludge it and you with his slimy secretions? Because you wanted him to notice you, silly. That was the plan, wasn't it? To get him to notice you? But he had to notice the dress first. Which he did. Then why are you so angry? You can buy another one just like it.

Because it was a gift. From my Oma.

My bottom lip quivers as tears gather along the edges of my eyelids. I snuffle, use a snot-soaked tissue to wipe away the gooey dredges hanging from my nose, shove my hand back into my lap where it rejoins its twin in worrying my hat. A sob dribbles from my mouth, rolls down my chin. I suck in a breath, clamp my teeth down, and purse my lips together. I run a quaking hand over the withered, patchy strands of my hair. A few stubborn, scarlet clumps mat the tangled locks, grabbing my trailing fingers, playing tug-of-war with the snarled ends.

They will be gone soon, before the sun fully rises, drawn back into the netherworld of hell that has become my mind.

I shudder. I use the blunt edge of a chipped and ragged knife blade to shuck the few remaining strands of hair from my tortured scalp. The flayed braids fall away, burn to red-tinged ash. They float away, free in their death.

I long for their freedom.

The clinging scents of rose and lilac shiver and die, stabbed through their hearts. They lay scattered in the grass at my feet, gasping their final breaths. A cloying stench hangs in the air, stroking the singed edges of my rancid whimsy.

Mein Liebling.

"Please, Oma. Not now."

Where have you been my love? We missed you.

Do I lie? No, she will know. She always knows. "With the Confessor of the Damned."

Ah. Confessing your sins?

"Confessing his."

Mein Liebling, Rosalinde. The desolate touch of a dead hand on my cheek. Calloused fingertips chafing my skin. *Why do you torture yourself? You can't change the past.*

I stiffen, flinching from the withered flesh. "If I had known the truth, I could have changed my path. I might have even known happiness." I look into empty and rotting eyes. "They took everything from me. And now I shall do the same. I can make them suffer in the same way they made me suffer."

A disappointed sigh, the breath drenched with decay and rot. *This is not how a promising young woman should behave. Your grandpapa and I did not raise you for this. For death.*

I wipe the tears from my eyes, smear mascara and eyeliner down my cheeks. "Ah, Oma," I say, wiping my nose with the back of a trembling hand. "I know now that you and Grandpapa did what you thought was best to protect me from our family curse, the pact our ancestor made with the demon."

A soft, mournful sigh. The tentative touch of rotted flesh.

I flinch from the stroke. "I know it was not your fault that I was doomed to this curse. You did your best. You hid me. Kept my hair shorn throughout my childhood into adolescence. Tried to protect me from the truth of what haunted me."

I pause, draw in a ragged breath and wipe away more tears gathering at the corners of my eyes. "But in the end, it was not enough." A moment of anger twists me into a knot. "You should have told me the truth. You should have trusted me with the truth."

It should have been enough. You were ours to protect. If your grandpapa hadn't allowed that witch to influence him with her empty promises and lies—

"It was not all Grandpapa's fault, now, was it?"

Silence. A held breath. The shake of a head, remorse glimmering from festering eyes. *Perhaps.*

A single, reluctant word. The closest I will ever come to receiving an apology. "Grandpapa did the best he could with what little you allowed him to share. He at least taught me how to survive."

He taught you how to become a killer.

"You should not have kept the truth from me, Oma. It was your lies that drove me into the arms of Mother Gothel, not Grandpapa's weaknesses."

Silence, embraced by a restlessness that not even death could calm.

A sad smile. I shake my head. Even the dead wore their pride as a badge of honor. "The Heralds of the Seventh Seal stole everything from me. Death and destruction are what I owe them in return. And I pay my debts."

I look into the slowly brightening morning, chewing my bottom lip, clenching back the flood of tears threatening to overwhelm the dam. The robins are silent; the chicks settled into their nests, their tummies full and content, nestling beneath their mothers, warm and safe.

What would that have felt like? How would life have blessed me if the mother I'd never known had been able to wrap me in that kind of love and gentle affection? With my papa by her side?

Would she have protected me from our curse better than my Oma? Or would I have sought the curse regardless? Taken hold of it as I have done now, knowing the consequences of that choice? Would I have chosen the path of justice or lived my life in quiet contentment as a wife and mother?

The shrill caw of a nearby crow shatters the uneasy silence.

I start and blink. "Oma?"

Come home soon, my beloved granddaughter.

Sniffling, I pull a worn and ragged ultrasound photo from the pocket of my blood-smeared sweater, brush trembling fingers across the bent, crinkled, and creased surface, and stare longingly at the indistinct and blurry images of my twin daughters, whom I named Abigail and Anna after my dead mother and her sister. They hug one another, nestling in the confined safety of my womb.

My heart stutters, longing and loss squeezing my chest.

Quiet laughter skips past me, carried in the gentle embrace of the early morning breeze.

I look up, folding and slipping the photo into my sweater pocket.

A man and a woman, their bodies pressing hip to hip, and linking arms, wander through the grassy field beyond the path and the bench where I sit. They bend their faces close together, gazes intent on each other, lips sprouting tender and loving whispers. The woman smiles and laughs. The man lowers his face to hers, kisses her. She strokes his cheek, takes his free hand and places it against the swell of her stomach.

I shudder, the breath catching in my throat. "Rosalinde Grimm is dead," I whisper into the morning air. "I am Rapunzel. Come to avenge what was taken from me."

Reality shifts and fades, my mind retreating from the present and into the past, peeling the rotting lid from the grief and rage entangling the shattered remains of my lost innocence.

Sheep's Clothing

ELEVEN YEARS EARLIER...

A horde of dust motes floated aimlessly upon seas of early afternoon sunlight that streamed in through open windows. The edges of drawn gauze curtains fluttered lazily in the gentle breeze that wandered into the kitchen. Outside, horses nickered nearby. They galloped around the perimeter of their corral, threw clotted dirt from their thundering hooves, tossed flowing manes proudly into the springtime air.

Across a mowed and trimmed grass field, cattle lowed, munched on newly grown alfalfa. Laughter drifted from the barn, accompanied by teasing words, shouted back-and-forth like canon volleys.

The heady scents of the freshly mown grass and alfalfa road the lazy wind, soft and silent in the sunlit heavens.

I stood in our kitchen, beside the closed door, clutching a pitcher of freshly squeezed lemonade to my chest. I held my breath, sure of my stealth as I listened to the voices swirling through our sun-drenched living room. Oma and Grandpapa sat together on our brown and tan leather couch, wizened bodies not quite touching, hands clenched in their separate laps.

Across from them, separated by the low standing maple coffee table between the couch and matching leather settee, sat Mother Miriam Gothel, Mother Superior of the Mission of Hope Home for Wayward and Unwanted Children, a veiled sanctuary established and operated by an unknown and secret church sect named the Heralds of the Seventh Seal.

When Oma had dismissed me to prepare refreshments and snacks for our guest, she drilled Grandpapa with an angry glare for inviting Mother Gothel into our home.

The reason for her visit?

Me.

My scalp itched beneath my closely shorn hair, the stubby ends of my locks pricking my fingertips. Hollow voices whispered through my thoughts, their coarse tones scraping my mind with dulled razor blades. The thorny points of my hair shivered, stretched outward into crisp warm air.

Our family curse, its black, putrid sting slowly dawning, the demons inside waking. The curse that Oma had protected me from during my childhood and as I began to grow into a woman.

Until she couldn't.

I shuddered, nearly dropped the pitcher of lemonade clutched to my chest when my hands forgot their duties, and sucked in a quick, panicked breath.

"Rosalinde?" Oma called.

I grasped the pitcher handle in a trembling hand, smoothed the front of my dress with the other. Shoving the door open, I stepped into the battlefield.

Oma and Grandpapa sat apart on the couch, old allies suddenly separated by the discovery of long-kept secrets and confidences be-trayed. Oma's gaze smoldered. Grandpapa leaned back into the couch, eyes cast downward, expression leaking chagrin and shame, cowed by Oma's ire.

Mother Gothel perched in the settee. She sat board stiff and straight, legs pinched together, hands folded primly within the embrace of her lap. She stared at Oma and Grandpapa, her thin lips pressed into a tight, severe line, her crooked nose like the beak of an eagle.

I cleared my throat.

Three pairs of eyes turned my way.

I offered the pitcher. "Lemonade?" I asked.

Mother Gothel smiled, the expression not quite reaching her eyes. She caught my gaze and held it, her expression firm, yet compassionate. Her eyes rose to my cropped curls.

"I would love a glass," she said, her voice laced with crushed gravel, her tone attempting kindness.

I glanced at Oma, handed a filled glass to our guest, poured two more glasses. Oma shook her head. Grandpapa reached for his glass, seemed to think better of it, leaned back into his hidey-hole.

"This is delicious!" Mother Gothel said. "Did you make this yourself, my dear?"

I lowered my gaze, bit my lower lip as I poured a glass for myself. "Yes, ma'am," I said.

She tried a second smile, abandoned the effort. "As I have tried to tell you, Annabelle, your husband did well to inform us of your granddaughter's...situation."

Oma bristled, shot an angry glare at Grandpapa. "There is no situation for you to be involved in," she said. "And my *husband*," she bit the word off as if she were snapping kindling for a fire, "consulted you without my knowledge or permission."

Mother Gothel swiveled her gaze toward me. "Then you are familiar with the demon curse affecting your family." She glanced at Oma. "And how to control it."

Oma blushed. "The curse affects the first-born daughter of every generation. Keeping their hair shorn—"

"Is at best a short-term and temporary solution," Mother Gothel said. "And one fraught with dangers as I am sure you are aware." She offered her hand to me. "Come, child. Sit next to me."

I looked at Oma, allowed Mother Gothel to pull me beside her. She smelled of citrus and lavender, but slightly sour, like a moldy peach or orange. She kept my hand in her lap, her skin rough and chapped.

"Tell me how you feel, child."

I hesitated, uncertain what I should say, what I should share. "I—"

"The girl feels nothing." Oma stood, teetered for an instant, before gaining her balance, physically and emotionally. She reached toward me. "Rosalinde."

Mother Gothel's grip on my hand tightened. For an instant, pain lanced through my fingers. "Tell your Oma what you are feeling," she said. "Tell her what you are hearing." A pause as she tapped the side of her head. "In here."

"Oma?" Fear wrenched my thoughts. I twisted my hand from Mother Gothel's grip and tried to stand. Agony pierced my mind. My legs buckled, tossed me back into the settee and Mother Gothel's quieting embrace. Whimpers staggered from between my lips, dribbled into my lap. I squeezed my eyes closed, grimaced as the spasm tore pieces of my thoughts from my mind. "Make it stop!" I pleaded. "Please make it stop!"

"Rosalinde!"

Mother Gothel hugged me, caressed my throbbing skull with a gentle hand until the shooting agony faded, and I was able to breathe once more.

"How old?" Mother Gothel asked.

"Fifteen," said Grandpapa.

Mother Gothel stroked my shorn hair and kissed my forehead, allowing me to lean back into the settee. "Past puberty," she said. "You are fortunate that the demons have not manifested before this. But they are manifesting now. And if you do nothing, they will consume the girl, your family, and everyone around you."

Tears glistened in Oma's eyes. She stifled a sob, glanced down at Grandpapa. "We...I...thought we could control it."

Mother Gothel smiled. "And you have. But puberty is dangerous. Once the child reaches adulthood, the only way to ensure her sanity and survival is to attempt to expel the demons."

"That will kill the curse?"

A shrug. "Unknown. Though the Heralds of the Seventh Seal are dedicated to eradicating demon possessions, curses such as this one that infects your family—" She paused. "It is something that will need time and vigilance to determine if removing the demons from Rosalinde will, in fact, end the curse."

"You can remove the demons from my mind?" I asked.

Mother Gothel stroked my head. "It will be difficult and will take time. And dedication from you. Once begun, we cannot stop until the process is completed. Do you understand?"

I nodded. "Oma?"

Tears rolled down her cheeks. She blew her nose into a well-worn linen handkerchief, shoved it into a coat pocket. "The decision is yours, child. I will not force you."

"Yes," I said. "If there is any chance that I can live without this curse."

Mother Gothel stood, her eyes gleaming, a self-satisfied smile twitching the corners of her mouth. "Then we shall proceed." She pulled me from the settee, hugged me and kissed my brow. One of our brethren, an initiate, whom we call A Novice of the Seal, will come for you tomorrow. His name is Eric." She turned to Oma and Grandpapa. "It is a difficult decision to trust the wellbeing of your child..." She gazed at me. "Or your grandchild with someone you do not know. But I assure you that I will take very good care of your Rosalinde and treat her as if she were my own daughter."

Forbidden Fruits

I SAT ON MY bed, my back pressed to the cold, dank wall in my basement cell, cloaked in eerie shadows. The undressed stone scuffed the skin beneath the silky thin fabric of my nightdress, picking at the healing scabrous lines crisscrossing my back, a lesson in humility and chasteness from Father Confessor Augustus Matthews.

I remembered Mother Gothel's disgust as I was dragged from the Father's reconciliation room. She squatted beside me, her rancid breath drifting through my blood-hazed agony. She dragged sweat tangled strands of hair from my eyes.

"Recalcitrant wretch," she hissed. "You were told that you were not meant for the Homestead boy. And yet..." She shook her head. "You have no idea what you have done, do you?" She peered into my eyes and frowned. "And you do not care."

She rose, glared down upon my misery, devoid of compassion or pity. "When it is time," she said. "You shall give us your children, and only then shall you be allowed to be with your beloved Eric. In death." A final scowl before she closed my cell door behind her.

I hugged my knees to my chest with shivering arms, ignored the whispered call of the lives growing in my womb. My children. Eric's children. Forbidden.

A single candle, its wax spent nearly to its roots, sputtered from the scraped and scarred lamp table squatting next to my bed. A trail of smoke wandered up from the wavering flame, disappearing into the cloying darkness above.

An unpretentious gown, the color of lavender on a warm spring day, lay at the foot of my bed, coyly inviting me to don it and luxuriate in its silken embrace. The armoire from which the dress had come, hunkered against the wall facing my bed. It stood in sullen silence, staring back at me from the gloom, pouting like an insolent and spoiled child.

Three lanterns hugged the curved walls of my chamber, their light snuffed and dead, though the means for me to light them lay beside the struggling candle. I had not the strength nor the will to trudge across the empty spaces to breathe life into their smoke-silted enclosures.

A muted fire licked at pine and cedar logs buried in the depths of cold, dark ash from the fireplace across my room. Sparks popped and sizzled as the dying flames scratched sap from the pine, lapping it up like a dying dog. The entwined stench of pine and cedar meandered through the air, tickling my nose with empty promises and broken oaths.

A shaft of argent moonlight speared through my uncurtained window, splashed across the debris-littered stone floor. Darkness gnawed at the edges of the moonlight.

A lone cricket, my only companion these past few days, chirped a forlorn song from the opposite corner of my chamber, its staccato beat thudding against my skull.

My scalp burned beneath the sprawling strands of my golden red hair, the tattered ends chafing the scuffed skin between my shoulder blades. Voices slithered through my thoughts, whispering nightmares of torment and torture.

I could not sleep.

But neither did I know when I was awake.

Monsters slid between the retreating moonlight and the darkness embracing my chamber. Their eyes glowed crimson in the night, dripping blood that sizzled and spit when it splat against the floor.

I shivered in my nightdress, eyes squeezed closed, praying to an uncaring god to make the voices stop.

"Eric, my love," I whispered into the dark. "Why have you abandoned me?"

Lunatic giggles answered my plea, their inharmonious melodies peeling back the skin from my disintegrating sanity. Wraithlike hands rattled the bars of their prison, buried deep within the confines of my rotting soul. The work of Mother Yasmina, Cardinal of Purification for the Heralds, and Mother Gothel's second-in-command. My curse restrained and trapped, but not yet exorcised, Yasmina's task left incomplete.

My thoughts staggered drunkenly through my mind, sopping up the puddles from my memories.

A face appeared before me. A frayed image of Mother Gothel during the first night of my captivity. She had sat beside my bed as I tossed and turned, pulled down into the inky depths of a drug-induced trance, my mind paralyzed and unable to lock away the demons slithering behind my unraveling thoughts. They burst forth from their crumbling prison, running amok, their incessant psychotic jabbering tossing fiery brands through the forest of consciousness, burning the trees to the ground.

I woke the next morning, drenched in sweat, shackled to my bedposts, the demons forced back into the cells and the doors locked, but now rusted and ramshackle. My entire body ached, cried out in alarm when I yanked against the cuffs binding my wrists and ankles.

Mother Gothel stood at the foot of the bedframe, hands clasped chastely at her waist, her demeanor no longer compassionate or caring, but edged with honed steel, razor-sharp, slicing away the layers of my naïve trust. Eric Homestead, the initiate who had brought me to the children's home, sat beside me, his hand firmly holding mine, yet with tenderness and compassion.

I tried to pull my hand from his, but his grip overpowered my bedraggled strength.

"The bonds were necessary," Mother Gothel said. "To protect you and us as we observed and evaluated you during the night."

"I want to go home," I said, my voice shivering with weakness.

Mother Gothel flinched an icy smile. "But you have just arrived."

"I thought—"

"You thought what?" she replied, her voice snapping the air bullwhip swift, the tip of her tone flaying open my stilted thoughts.

I cringed. "I—"

"And what shall you do when you return home?" she asked, her tone forged in iron. "Continue as you have until neither you nor your grandmother can contain the demons inside your soul and they are released?"

She paused, her unforgiving gaze hammering at me, forcing me to envision the death and the destruction that awaited us if I abandoned the Heralds of the Seventh Seal now, before they had the chance to exorcise the demons from me and kill the curse that infected my soul.

"Did your grandmother ever tell you what happened to your mother and father?"

I shook my head. Eric's hold on my hand intensified.

"Anna, your aunt, refused to acknowledge the truth of your family's curse. She refused to believe it to be real and so did nothing to try and control it until it was too late and she, your mother, and your father were dead."

I stared, mute, as the horror of what she described played across the rambling stage of my thoughts.

"Is that what you wish for you and your grandparents?"

I shook my head.

The flint grasping Mother Gothel's face softened. "Good," she said as she slid around to the other side of my bed and took my other hand. "You need to be brave and steadfast if you hope to rid yourself of the demons possessing your soul. As I told you before, the rites we must perform to drive the demons from you are not without risk. To us or to you. But it is the only way. If you hope to survive and live a full and rich life."

Her gaze held my own, the intensity in her eyes chiseling away the remaining pebbles of my resistance.

"Is that what you wish?"

I nodded, my voice still hiding and fearful.

"Good." She glanced at Eric. A look passed between them, vanishing before I could comprehend its meaning. "Eric will be your companion during your time here. Like you, he came to us possessed by a family curse. After we cleansed him of the demons infesting his soul, he chose to remain and join our cause."

A soft knock upon my door dragged me from my tortured musings. I wiped away the tears staining my cheeks. "Eric?"

A key rattled in the lock. The door opened. Garish lantern light spilled through the opening.

I held my breath, hope igniting for an instant.

Mother Yasmina, my piecemeal exorcist, slipped through and closed the door quietly behind her. She stood still and silent for a breath, held her lantern aloft as she scanned my prison.

Hope died, the spark smothered. "Go away," I said. "Leave me alone."

She hissed, crossed the emptiness between us, snagged the gown languishing at the foot of my bed and tossed it at me. "We have no time for your self-pity," she said. "If you do not escape now, Gothel shall have your children, and you will spend eternity buried beneath the bowels of this accursed place." She stared, held the lantern up, its light tossing back the shadows clinging to my bleak mood.

I shoved the gown from me, curled into a tighter ball of grim anguish.

Muttering curses in Latin, she thrust the gown back at me, and, grasping my arm, yanked me from the bed. "Dress. Now," she ordered. "Unless it is your true desire to languish in this prison until your children are delivered and you are thrown out with the rest of the offal."

I met her glare, my desperation fueling my sparking anger. "Where is Eric?" I asked.

Mother Yasmina spat more curses in Latin. "It is too late for him," she said. "Now dress yourself, or I shall do it for you." Without waiting for my response, she crossed back to the door, cracked it open, and peered through.

"I will not leave without him."

She spun around, anger, fear, and panic warring across her shriveled face. "Stupid girl. You would undo us all."

I threw the gown down and crossed my arms. "Then we shall, all of us, fall."

The crack of a grimace. Hesitation as the thoughts and plans scuttled across her expression. Lips pursed, she nodded. "Hurry," she said and slid back out the door.

Innocence Shattered

I SAT UPON ERIC'S bed in his tower chamber, dressed in the satin gown Mother Yasmina had forced upon me. Its warm and inviting lavender shades favored my emerald eyes and my hastily combed golden red tresses. Thankfully, the demon voices inside my soul were silent and sleeping. A borrowed down comforter surrounded me where I sat, rumpled into an anxious embrace.

A fire burned in the hearth, the yellow-red flames dancing, popping, and snapping, their usual soothing voices agitated and anxious. A bouquet of Rapunzel that I had picked from the garden and given to my beloved lounged in a scarred and scratched glass vase hunkering upon a weathered wooden mantel, the delicate violet petals beginning to wilt.

Pale yellow light guttered from the lanterns bolted to the stone walls. Wisps of oily smoke wafted upward, their stringy spirals vanishing into the shadows embracing the smoke-littered whitewashed ceiling. Like the ceiling of my own chamber I had come to fear and loathe in the years since my thralldom to Mother Gothel and her insidious machinations.

Oma and Grandpapa suspiciously dead within a month of my captivity. The local authorities indifferent and apathetic. My ancestral home broken up and sold off. Ensuring I had nowhere to run, no one to trust.

The witch owned me.

Tears streaked my face, gathered at the cleft of my chin before raining sodden drops into the fabric of my gown. I buried my shaking hands chastely into the folds of my lap, resisted my burgeoning desire to reach out to Eric, my lover and confidant, as he paced the floor of the room, his shined black leather boots tapping the cedar planks, their staccato beat echoing off the chiseled stone.

Worry creased his lean, beard-stubbled face, his brows drawn down to his dusty blue eyes. He didn't seem to know what to do with his hands. They swung restlessly at his sides for a few marching steps, shackled themselves behind his tensed back as he turned at the round-ed corner of the chamber and retraced his troubled parade.

He stopped beside me and stared. The distress burning behind his eyes frightened me.

"Are you sure?" he asked. "Mother Gothel said this to you, that she will have our child as penance for our disobedience?"

I chewed my lower lip to prevent it from trembling. I nodded as I dragged my hands to the tiny swell of my stomach. "Must I show you the bloody stripes crisscrossing my back to make you believe the truth behind my words?"

He stared.

I drew in a shaking breath. "You did not visit me for several weeks, so I could not tell you. And even if I could, I did not know if you would—"

"What?" he snapped. Regret at his sudden harshness softened the apprehension glaring from his eyes. He sighed and sat beside me, wrapped me in his tender embrace as the sobs wracked my body. He smoothed the errant curls from my tear-stained face, brushed my lips with his own.

"It's not your fault," he said. "We both were eager participants. And I shall never abandon you. Never!"

His smile chased back the gloom cloaking us.

"Do you believe me?" he asked.

I sniffled and nodded, wiped my nose and cheeks with a soggy handkerchief. "I do," I said.

He kissed my cheek and stood, resumed his frenetic pacing, stopped before the fire, and pounded the mantel with his fist, causing the Rapunzel to shiver in its disfigured prison.

A sudden flaming glint burst from his gaze. He shook his head, pulled me from the bed.

"We cannot wait," he said. "We must leave. Now, before Mother Gothel can contrive a means to prevent our escape." He paused, terrified shadows sliding past his eyes. "If we do not, Mother Gothel will have our child."

"But—" I began, horror clutching my throat. "What of Mother Yasmina?" I asked. "She said to wait for her return. Without her, we cannot hope to escape."

He didn't answer my questions but instead dragged me toward the chamber door. "No buts," he said. "No delays. We cannot wait for Yasmina's return. She may already be undone and a prisoner of Mother Gothel. We must leave. Now."

The chamber door shuddered. A shoulder pounded the iron-bound oak beams. It shook once more, exploded inward, raining Eric's room with savage, knife-edged splinters.

Father Confessor Augustus Matthews breached the sudden opening, a cudgel gripped in his hand, fiery intent blazing from his eyes.

He stormed into the room, murder contorting his face as he scanned the room. He charged Eric, his club swinging in a lethal arc meant to crush in the side of my beloved's skull.

Eric ducked, avoided the killing stroke, but was not swift enough to dodge a second blow that spun him top-like into the wall. He smashed into the hand-chiseled stone, tried to turn. Father Matthews slammed a fist into the side of Eric's face. He collapsed into a heap, blood streaming from his broken nose and shattered cheek. His gaze met mine as he struggled to rise, fell in on himself, and convulsed.

Light glinted off polished steel from the floor in front of the hearth.

Eric's knife. Lost in his struggle with Matthews.

I stumbled toward my lover.

Father Confessor Matthews blocked my path.

I evaded his grasp, sunk to the floor, and grasped the knife as night's darkness cloaked the room, sucking the life from the gasping air. The Father gripped my arm in a crushing grasp, yanked me to my feet. I slashed the knife blade across his cheek. He grunted, stepped back, but snagged my wrist before I could complete the return stroke and twisted my arm. Stabbing pain bayoneted me. My fingers opened, dropping the knife. I followed, clattering to the floor beside it, scooping it into the disarray surrounding me as Mother Gothel strode through the doorway.

Rage engulfed her. She stopped within the threshold, her wrath sweeping the room. Her ire settled on Eric. "Is this how you repay me for my kindness?" she asked. "With betrayal?" She stepped into the room. "We gave you everything and in return asked only one thing." Frenzy and fury chased across her thin face, twisting her expression into a horrific mask. "You were supposed to watch her, and nothing more. You were not meant for her." Her gaze swept over me. "And yet, in your hubris you thought you could steal her and her seed from us.

A sin you shall pay seventy times seven for. And when we are finished, you will beg for more than death, a mercy we will not grant."

Eric returned her glare, heaved a stuttering breath.

Darkness engulfed me.

I looked up.

Mother Gothel stood over me, eyes blazing with outrage. "Mother Yasmina will not be coming back for you and your...gigolo."

My hope sputtered and died, its empty husk scattered by the hurricane gales blowing from Mother Gothel's ire. "And your children," she said, "shall be the penance for your sin."

"Children?"

The shocked astonishment in Eric's slurred voice twisted my gut.

Mother Gothel snorted. "Twins," she said, her voice shoving the knife into Eric's chest and twisting it through his heart. She smiled. "You were not aware."

The heat of Eric's bewildered stare burned through my terror. I glanced at him, swallowing chagrin and dread.

"How long..." His breath stuttered. "How long have you known?"

I managed a shrug, tears spilling down my cheeks, as I protected my womb with shaking hands, Eric's knife hidden within the folds of my gown.

His gaze slid from my tear-blurred eyes to my womb and back. He screamed, launched himself into the hulking man standing over him. The top of his skull cracked into the Father's chin. He staggered back, dropped his cudgel. Eric folded to his knees, reached for the club. Blood clotted his hair, streamed down over his eyes.

Mother Gothel stepped toward him, rammed the toe of her boot into his chest.

Eric crumpled to the floor, clutching his chest. Mother Gothel stepped toward him, drove her boot into his ribs. He screamed, curled into a ball, agony contorting his broken and bloody face.

Scowling down at him, her eyes blazing with maniacal glee, she then drove her boot heel into the side of his skull.

Blood burst from Eric's mouth and nose, splattered the flagstones, slapped the side of my face with goo.

At a nod from Mother Gothel, Father Augustus heaved Eric up by the collar of his jacket, dragged him to the open chamber window, and tossed him through the gaping maw into the whipping sleet.

I screamed, flung myself into Mother Gothel, driving the knife blade into her chest, and burying it to the hilt.

She gasped, tore herself from my convulsing grasp, and collapsed against the wall, her hands snatching at the knife handle. Blood seeped through the gold and silver silk brocade embroidering the deep blue fabric of her bodice. She sank to the floor, her eyes spewing virulence and rage.

The Father Confessor hesitated, his gaze shifting from me to Mother Gothel and back, uncertainty shimmering behind his eyes.

I fled, smearing the blood from my hands down my gown as I lurched down the winding stairs, through the hallway and gallery, into the howling teeth of the freezing wind and oblivion.

Hell's Wrath

I HAD ALWAYS LOVED late spring in northern Colorado. Pink and white cherry blossoms, the tree limbs fluttering in the breeze. The scent of lilac wafting in the air. The cloying aroma of freshly mown grass. The shrill, cacophonous chirping of robins from the trees in the early morning before the sun rose. The smell of freshly baked bread from my Oma's oven strolling through our ranch house, crooked finger inviting me from my bed to the kitchen. There, I would enjoy a warm, soft chunk torn from a steaming loaf, slathered with butter and homemade peach preserves from last year's crop of Palisade peaches before following my grandpapa into the barn for our morning chores.

That life vanished on my fifteenth birthday, when Oma and Grandpapa allowed Mother Miriam Gothel to take me from my home and into the embrace of the Heralds of the Seventh Seal with empty promises to purge me of the demons possessing my soul and end the curse that had haunted our family for four centuries.

Two years later, I barely escaped with my life in the midst of a snarling autumn snowstorm from Clear Butte, the Heralds, and Mother Gothel, my beloved Eric, murdered.

Now, thirty-one weeks pregnant with our twins, my golden red hair shorn and carefully styled into a pixie cut, adorned with talismans to mute the demon voices stirring inside, I strolled through a Fort Collins city park. Traversing dew-blanketed grass between manicured gravel paths, I imagined my cherished Eric by my side, our hands entwined. I did my best to live a quiet and unassuming life, but never felt comfortable or entirely safe, always looking over my shoulder, expecting to see Mother Gothel.

Above, a swath of midnight blue velvet gazed down from the remnants of the cloudless day. The park lights cast a mellow white glow, accentuating winding avenues of purple sage, tangled jungles of multi-colored snapdragons, Rocky Mountain columbine, and scarlet paintbrush.

Crickets chirped a soothing melodic symphony.

I smiled, my mind lost in memories wrapped in ribbons and fantastical paper glinting in soft firelight as if it were Christmas again and I was opening my presents from under the tree. I pictured my fingers wrapped around Eric's, their grip tightening ever so slightly as he leaned in to kiss my lips. A hollow and bittersweet memory at best.

My gaze slid across the emptiness surrounding me, probed the chaotic lines of blue spruce and pine dotting the path. Their needle-heavy limbs swayed hypnotically in the gentle evening late spring breeze, muting the dimming swath of orange and flaming red brushing the dimming western sky. The muffled creak of slender tree trunks floated upon the warm air, dulling the apprehension and anxiety that constantly clung to my thoughts.

Abigail and Anna kicked and squirmed within my womb, their sisterly tussle yanking my troubled imaginings into the present.

I closed my eyes and smiled as I dreamt of Eric squeezing my hand and leaning toward me to whisper, *I love you*, his peppermint-scented breath tickling my ear. I shivered and grinned like the fool I believed myself to be, wondering how I had become part of this man's life amid the stifling dread that had embraced us in Mother Gothel's world.

For a heartbeat, the terrors of those memories faded.

In my thoughts, I reached up and stroked his cheek with trembling fingers. He took my hand and kissed it before laying it upon my belly. I imagined one twin kicking at his touch. I cringed. Eric laughed, delight flashing through his deep blue eyes. He stopped, knelt on the path before me, and kissed my stomach, whispered words I could not hear. The twins, however, responded in turn, tiny feet pressing against my womb, pushing against gentle fingers touching their home.

A dead branch snapped.

The night air sputtered.

Eric vanished from my wistful thoughts.

The rasping trees fell silent and still. Their limbs drooped with sudden exhaustion.

A breath dragged in and held.

Shadowed forms emerged from the deeper, clinging darkness between the trees.

I stopped and stared, my heart hammering my chest, my hand clutching the absent knife I had used to stab Mother Gothel in the chest.

The twins fell silent.

I wished for Eric to appear, his body taut and coiled like a spring ready to snap, to protect me from the men that stood on the path before me.

But he did not appear. I was alone.

Soft footsteps behind, cutting off all thoughts of escape.

I looked back, and to the sides, settled my gaze upon the cloaked figure materializing from the darkness that blanketed the path.

Trepidation knotted my chest, snatched the breath from my lungs.

Mother Gothel lowered her hood. Her eyes blazed. Rot and corruption tingled the stagnate air. She smiled thinly, her gaze flicking to my belly, her expression lustful and greedy. "Bless you, my daughter, for you have sinned. Greatly. For which you have never atoned." She nodded.

A hulking shadow appeared at my side. Leather gloved hands rose to lower a sable cotton hood. Father Confessor Sebastian Oldham leered down at me.

"What's going on?" An unfamiliar voice belonging to a man, his tone challenging but distressed. Dressed in trendy running pants and tee shirt, he materialized from the shadows cloaking the path at the edge of the trees, his expression twisted with fear and confusion.

I pulled in a shaking breath, hoped the man would flee and not be brave.

My hope was crushed.

Branches snapped. Dead pine needles cracked. A grunt of surprise. Chased by fear.

Rooted by terror, I watched as a Knight of St. Michael, a member of Mother Gothel's foot soldiers, flung the man into a nearby tree. Branches jerked, rained pine needles from the blackened canopy. Polished steel flashed. Blood sprayed. The man jerked, his hands clutching at his throat, blood soaking his tee-shirt, his mouth contorting into a silent scream as he crumbled to the ground, twitching and gasping like a landed fish.

Hands grasped my arms and dragged me forward.

Mother Gothel studied me, her gaze settling on my swollen belly. "It is time for you to confess, my daughter, and to pay your penance."

Penance

I screamed and thrashed, biting and clawing at the grasping nitrile-gloved hands pressing my shoulders down and pinning my flailing arms against the clammy caress of a bone-chilling metal table. My wrists were strapped down, the leather restraints snugged to strangle the blood flow from my wrists.

Twisting agony knotted my body, curled crushing fists through my bulging belly as Mother Gothel forced my legs apart. Leather shackles garroted my ankles in the birthing stirrups. My body jerked. Spasms cascaded through me. Shrieking, I snapped upward against the tethers, back arching. I fell back, panting. Sweat streamed off me, slicking the metal through my gown.

"Eric!" I screamed. "Where are you? Why did you leave me? You promised to be with me!" Memory slid the blade of a boning knife through my heart and into my soul. Eric was dead, his skull crushed beneath Mother Gothel's boot, then tossed through his open chamber window by Father Confessor Augustus Matthews.

Razor-edged spear points stabbed through my abdomen as my body corkscrewed through a muscle-rending contraction. I howled, thrashed against the leather manacles tethering me to the table. A hand probed the inside of my womb, searching.

A grunt of approval.

Mother Gothel's face appeared between my spread legs, a satisfied leer splitting her maw. "It will not be long," she crooned. "But you must try to relax. Otherwise, you may damage your daughters before they enter the world."

Ice clutched my thundering heart. A new round of contractions pounded my body, twisting and turning, wringing the strength from my limbs. I clenched my jaw against the rending agony. The spasms passed. I collapsed against the table. A dead chill seeped through the cotton membrane of my hospital gown. I felt sweat pooling on my forehead and face, dribbling down the sides of my head, slicking the sweaty table surface. My chest heaved, shoveling desperate breaths to and from my struggling lungs.

Rhythmic whispers sliced through my scattered thoughts. A rhyme from my earliest childhood memories. My skull tingled, crawled, spidery legs dancing a staccato beat against the bone. Fear and rage blossomed, pummeled my mind. I lurched upward, back bowing, threatening to snap my spine. Torment reared my muscles.

I screamed.

The leather straps crushing my wrists tore.

Curses littered the air.

Grasping hands grappled for my flailing hands.

Spears stabbed through my scalp, tearing and ripping. Golden red hair mushroomed, shimmering strands writhed, reached into the broiling shadows, twisting and twirling into thicker vine-like tendrils, the needled ends whipping the air into a frenzied froth.

I screamed, the agony bayoneting my mind and shredding tattered sanity into blood-crusted strips.

I tore an arm free, raked ragged nails across a lean, unfocused face, yowling into the sudden fury it spat back into me. Other hands snatched my thrashing arm and slammed it onto the table, pressed it down with bone-snapping strength as new leather bound me against the table.

My screamed curses rattled the close walls, echoed through the dingy, wavering light skinning the rough-chiseled cavern walls. Garish shadows danced frenetically, leering and jabbing darkness at me as I battled the demons pulling themselves from the detritus of my shredded soul.

A man, his face hidden beneath a surgical mask, howled, reeled back, blood-spattered hands clutching his face, crimson oozing between his fingers, the spiked ends of my jerking and twisting hair splattering vermillion froth over the nearby wall.

A voice rose above the chaotic din, chanting power and vehemence.

The torment thundering through my head quivered as if struck through the heart by a blue-hot arrow tip. The hurricane thrashing my hair died, its outrage stolen. My locks fell, hung limp and lifeless from my scalp.

Hands grasped my head in a vise-like grip, slammed it down onto the table, rattling my teeth. Black spots danced through my eyes, blotted out the wavering light, carried me down into a shrinking, lightless tunnel.

I tasted blood.

Leather suddenly strained against my forehead, pressed into my flesh and bone, snugging a coarse and scratchy road around my head. More hands clutched my jaw, forced it open, shoved hardened rubber into my mouth.

I bit down, grinding teeth into the rocklike surface.

Searing pain blazed through me.

Torchlight glinted off flashing steel, touched fire to my scalp. My hair dropped in flaming, tangled knots, slithering a torturous dance across the stone floor for a breath, shivered and died.

My body clenched, muscles straining to purge the two lives from my womb. I strained against the urge, but it was too late.

Tears streaked the sides of my face. Pain pulsed and throbbed, threading glowing needles through my nerves. My body contracted. Muscles shoved and convulsed. I screamed as my body tore itself in two. I felt something slide from me, wet and boneless. My strength spent, I collapsed and spewed into the muck caressing me.

Another spasm. My body shoved. I was torn in two once more as a second pulpy mass slithered from my womb.

I panted, licked dried and cracked lips.

A pair of ear-splitting, plaintive cries echoed through the cavern.

My heart lurched, my torment forgotten in the instant that love blossomed, reaching out into the void for my babies.

A face materialized. Aged and withered, sun-scorched skin tanned into cracked and frayed leather, wrinkled and creased, the dim memory of beauty clinging to the furrows. A slender nose, perhaps once straight, now bent and broken. Pinched, bloodless lips that had borne more loss than love. Wiry silver-gray hair curled into long, lanky tangled brambles nestled beside her bony skull, light glinting from the twitching ends.

Mother Gothel, her mask momentarily laid aside and forgotten.

Eyes cold and calculating, smoldering with an icy intensity, pulsating coals glowing orange behind the glinting platinum. The hint of desiccated compassion.

Her gaze held me, drained my resistance, left me bereft and panting with fatigue, unable to fight the scorching needles continuing to sear through me.

She reached out with a parched hand, spindly fingers trembling the air between us, stroked my cheek, a knife-like nail flicking a stray tear from the side of my face.

A compassion-gutted smile. She leaned over, pressed her mouth to my ear, whispered dry, brittle words, her breath like fallen leaves on a cold autumn morning.

"You were warned of the consequences," she said. "And now is the time of your reckoning." She straightened. "Your lifelong penance for your sins has begun." She retrieved my babies, held them up into the guttering light for me to see, a desolate smile twisting her emaciated mouth. "So that you shall know the price of your sin and folly."

I whimpered, then shouted, thrashing against the leather straps binding me to the table as the darkness grappled for my mind and yanked me into the abyss.

Fragments

Shadows and light.

Bodies stood at the edges of sight. Watching.

I reached out to them, but they stepped away, their faces hidden. I called to them. They hesitated before turning back.

Darkness intruded, sweeping past the light, snuffing life. Hope struggled, battered and beaten by the starless black. It faded and withered. The figures struggled against the blackness. They stood for an instant before being swept away in the hurricane.

I reached out to them, panic twisting and turning, coiling around my heart tighter and tighter. I shouted to them, my hope charring to ash. My hand fell as I was dragged back. One body fought against the maelstrom, tore through the veil, thrust a shaking hand toward me. Behind the hand stared Eric, his eyes blank and empty, expression numb, face slack. Blood seeped from the crevices and cracks of his crushed skull and his broken and mangled body.

Demon's eyes hovered beside Eric's broken figure, glowing with disease and dripping blood. A festering, gangrenous arm snaked out from the darkness. Long, sinuous fingers sprouting razor-edged talons wrapped around the side of his face, punctured sagging flesh and shattered bone. The demon laughed, its feral eyes spearing my soul with its malevolence as it yanked Eric back into the black void of nothingness.

I screamed.

Razor-edged colorless light blinded me. The vague outline of a sterile and empty room appeared. Rapid and clipped beeps thumped my skull. Keen-edged pain lanced my body. Dry, chapped lips stuttered silent, incomprehensible words.

I could hear hushed, murmuring voices surrounding me. Quiet, anxious, rasping and harsh. A muffled gasp.

Silence followed.

The fog cleared. Lines, edges, and corners gained perspective: White, antiseptic light drizzled down from a chalky and featureless ceiling. Disinfected air wandered the empty spaces, kissed my face with immaculate and unsoiled lips.

I shivered.

A face materialized from the flawless gleam surrounding me.

A woman, face lean, expression stern, brown, gray-streaked hair pulled tightly back into a severe bun, her square, featureless body stuffed inside a long, white coat. A miniature diamond pendant winked uncertainly above the collar of a powder-blue blouse.

She tried on an emotionless smile, discarded it in favor of an austere look.

"Miss?"

Her voice scraped my frayed nerves.

I blinked, turned my gaze from the woman to a man standing behind her. His face sagged with grief-ridden gloom, eyes bruised and haunted. They met my stare for an instant, slid away.

He cleared his throat, a practiced, yet uneasy sound. Discomfort rode his shoulder, leaned into his ear, muttering. The man closed his eyes and shuddered, his chest quivering with unease and restlessness.

"Miss."

The woman again. I didn't like her voice, but was drawn to it, a moth to the flame. I looked at her and blinked.

She leaned over me, her breath minty, yet slightly rancid. "Can you hear me? Do you understand me?"

I nodded, swallowed my burgeoning trepidation. "Where am I?" The coarse, gnarled quality of my voice caused me to wince.

Hesitation.

"You're in the hospital. White Willow Medical Center."

The name sounded familiar. An institution plucked from my past and dropped into my lap.

I was back in Clear Butte.

"You've been unconscious for several days. You were—"

Alarm. My chest tightened, clinging to the breath in my lungs, unwilling to let it go. I strained against the rising hysteria, thrust the air out. My chest heaved. "Eric...where is my beloved?" My hand slid down to my flattened stomach. A tiny bulge pushed against the sheet and blanket, but it was not enough. Not nearly enough. "Where are my babies?" I cried.

The woman touched my shoulder in a soothing gesture. "Please," she said. "I need you to calm down."

I shook her hand off, struggled to rise, fell back, panting and gasping for breath. "Where are my babies?"

The woman grabbed a syringe from a nearby tray, pushed the needle into an IV port.

A stinging cold ran into my arm, spreading through my shoulder and chest. My panic slowed, grew lethargic, and vanished, smothered beneath the blanket of drug-induced calm. I sighed and settled back into my bed, dreamy thoughts rolling sluggishly through my mind.

The voices hidden within the depths of my rotting soul whispered and hissed, rattled chains and shackles. "Leave me alone," I whispered, my voice hoarse with desperation.

The woman's face appeared above me, drowned out the rest of the room in my view. She frowned, stroked my forehead with a motherly gesture. The voices quieted as the drugs pulled me further into their foggy well.

"That's better," she said. "How do you feel?"

"I—" the word slurred from my mouth, rolled off my chin and onto my blanket.

"Can you tell me your name?"

"Grimm," I muttered before I could think to say otherwise.

A muttered curse.

The man pushed past the woman. He grasped the bed railing, a fresh, gaping wound blazing through his eyes. The woman grabbed his arm. He shook her hand off.

"Rosalinde Grimm?" His intense stare pinned me down, pushed through the syrupy goo griming my thoughts, demanding an answer.

I swallowed back the lump lodged in my throat and nodded.

Another muttered curse. The man closed his eyes and pursed his lips. When he opened his eyes once more, they seemed to glow with a manic determination. "Miss Grimm," he said. "Rosalinde." He paused, sucked back his own grief. "My name is William Locke. I'm a detective with—"

The woman interrupted. "Detective, please," she said. "Not now. You need to leave."

He snarled. "If not now, when?" He turned back, his hands white, knuckling the bed railing. "Can you tell me what happened to your grandparents?"

"They're dead," I said, my voice slurring slightly.

"Did you kill them?" he said. "Did you burn down their home?"

I shook my head. "Mother Gothel—"

He frowned. "Who—?"

I gaped at him, hands trembling above the absent swell of my stomach. "Where are my babies? Where's Eric?"

"Detective!" the woman hissed at him. Anger squeezed her expression, dripped from her flinty gaze.

He brushed her indignation aside. "I'm sorry," he said, clamping his mouth closed as he gulped in a breath, his body tensing. He licked his lips, leaned over to consume my world. "Who's Eric?" he asked. "Your boyfriend?" His fists rattled the bed rail. "Did Eric kill your grandparents?"

I managed to push out a garbled laugh. I met his glare for a heartbeat and a breath, turned away, unable to endure his pain. I shook my head, whispered, "Eric is dead. She killed him."

"Who killed him? Who killed Eric? Rosalinde, what happened?"

His desperation drove a spike into my heart. I shook my head. "Eric tried to stop her. He wanted to take me away from her, take us both away from her. But she found out about us. She killed my beloved, but I escaped. I thought I was safe, but she found me."

"Rosalinde! Who found you? Was it your grandmother? Did she find out that you were pregnant, and that Eric was the father? Did she try to stop you from leaving with Eric?" He paused, scraped a hand through his hair, his expression twisting with imagined possibilities. "They argued, didn't they? Your grandmother and Eric. Things got out of hand, and Eric killed her. For you. For you both."

"No," I mumbled.

"It was an accident, wasn't it? Eric didn't mean to kill your grandmother or your grandfather. It was self-defense. And you just wanted to protect Eric. Hey, I get it. I understand. Tell me where you buried his body."

"I didn't...she killed my Oma and Grandpapa. She killed Eric because he tried to take me away. But I wasn't meant for him, so she said that I had to give her my babies, but I escaped. I thought I was safe, but she found me and brought me back." I closed my eyes and shook my head. My body trembled, my hands kneading the blanket over my flattened stomach. "She took my babies."

"Detective!"

The bed railing shook. Whiskey-tinged breath washed over me.

"Rosalinde, a game warden found you lying unconscious and bleeding on the side of a remote forest service road five days ago. It looked like you'd been there for several hours. Can you tell me what happened? Who left you there?"

The fog engulfing my mind grew thicker. It dragged me downward into the darkness. I fought to stay in the light, bit the inside of my cheek, the sudden stinging pain shredding the haze. Chains clanked and clattered from the bottom of the cesspool of my soul.

"Rosalinde! I need you to stay awake!"

The fierceness of his voice dragged me from my rising hysteria. I opened my eyes. "Where are my daughters?"

He slapped the bed rail, stepped back, ran a shaking hand through his thinning hair. He pursed his lips, frustration contorting his face. "Who took your babies?"

"I told you," I said. "Mother Gothel took my babies. She killed my grandparents, and she killed my beloved." The fog returned, thicker and stronger. My thoughts wandered, stumbled and fell. "Where are my babies?" I asked.

"Your babies are gone," he said. "What did you do with them?"

I gaped at him.

The doctor pulled him from my side. They huddled near the door, spoke in hushed, angry tones. The man glanced at me, anger and frustration warring across his face.

Madness and torment shattered my thoughts, scattering in a billion shards across the desolation of my heartbreak and misery.

My mind snapped.

A woman screamed.

A man shouted curses.

My world burned to ash.

Mother Gothel

Detective Locke

Mission of Hope Home for Wayward and Unwanted Children

William Locke braked his car beside an aged aluminum faced call box encased in a weathered and chipped brick enclosure that made the tin man from the Wizard of Oz look shiny and new. He stared at the vinyl billboard-sized sign leering down at him from over spiked wrought iron gates. Beyond the gates, the graded and smoothed dirt road meandered down a gentle slope and disappeared through a rambling stand of pine and blue spruce.

Cotton-teased clouds rolled through the afternoon sky, chased by their ragged shadows, the tattered edges scraping across a rolling landscape flooded with colorful wildflowers and tall, disheveled and tousled grasses. In the distance, at the bottom of the slope, the pine and spruce seemed to wave at him, inviting him to come down and join their party.

He glanced at himself in the rearview mirror, resisting the urge to touch the angry bruise clutching his right eye and the stitched gash racing across his forehead. He shuddered, remembering the rage and the violence when Rosalinde Grimm just...snapped. How she flew from her bed, screaming and howling, tossing medical equipment across the room, and nearly strangling her doctor before he and three security guards managed to pry the diminutive and scrawny girl off the woman.

She'd slipped from their grasp before they could subdue her, managed to rake her nails across one guard's face, and smash her patient monitor into Locke as the two remaining guards dog piled her to the floor.

He shivered, tried to erase the horror he saw twisting her face, the feral ferocity of her gaze as she bashed the monitor into the side of his head, knocking him down.

What he had seen terrified him.

Her panic, outrage, and fury when the judge dismissed her claims and committed her to Sacred Heart Psychiatric Hospital had horrified him more.

He thought of Olivia on the night she began her breakneck spiral into insanity the week before she drowned their two children and shot herself.

They'd argued. He'd said something stupid and cruel. She'd stared at him with that same feral look in her eyes as Rosalinde Grimm before locking herself in their bathroom. He remembered the rage...and the fear in her voice as she screamed and cried from the other side of the bathroom door. His horrified shock after kicking in the door at what she'd done to herself. Her head shaved, her scalp scraped, cut, and bleeding like the aftermath of a brutal battle.

Like Rosalinde Grimm.

He'd put her on a seventy-two-hour suicide watch at Sacred Heart Psychiatric Hospital, believed what the doctors told him about her condition when they discharged her. They'd all been horribly wrong.

Locke shuddered, slammed his hands into the steering wheel, forcibly purging the memories and the images from his mind.

He rolled down his window, punched the intercom button, noticed the security camera spying on him from the top of a spiked fence post.

The speaker cackled static. "Yes?"

"Detective Locke, Clear Butte PD, to see Mother Gothel. I have an appointment."

More static marching from the speaker.

He waited, glanced at the file in the seat beside him, his unsettled thoughts chewing on what he had managed to pry from Rosalinde Grimm before her mind blew itself apart, and her hospital room with it.

The discovery of the bodies of Annabelle and Harold Grimm in the burned-out ruins of their ranch house north of Clear Butte almost three years ago. Both had been shot in the back of the head with a small caliber weapon before the house was torched. Their missing fifteen-year-old granddaughter, Rosalinde Grimm, their primary suspect.

Discovering that their Jane Doe found bleeding and disoriented on the side of a remote back road was Rosalinde had been a sheer stroke of good luck. But where had she been for the past three years? She'd obviously been pregnant and had survived what looked like a back-alley birth. Locke suspected that Rosalinde's 'Eric' was the father.

But who was Eric?

An exhaustive search for missing persons from the area surrounding Fort Collins with the first name 'Eric' had returned a single hit. Eric Homestead. Age seventeen. Missing from Windsor four years ago, the bodies of his parents discovered in their home four days after neither reported to their jobs by a neighbor who smelled something rotting inside the Homestead house and called the police.

Thomas and Susan Homestead had been shot in the back of the head with a small caliber weapon, after which, the perpetrator had severed a natural gas line in an attempt to set the house on fire, but something had gone wrong, and the fire never started. Their son, Eric, had vanished. With no other leads or suspects, investigators concluded that Eric had killed his parents and fled.

Ballistics were inconclusive, but the investigating detective believed the bullets to have been fired from either a thirty or thirty-two caliber weapon.

With no other leads or witnesses, the case went cold.

Unfortunately for Locke, the fire that had destroyed the Grimm ranch house had been so intense that the bullets recovered from the scene had been rendered useless.

With no physical evidence to compare, except for the similarity of the murders, and the two missing teens, he had nothing he could use to connect the two crimes.

But he had a name. Mother Gothel. The name that Rosalinde kept repeating when asked who had taken her children and killed her 'Eric.'

After some digging, Locke discovered who he believed was Rosalinde's Mother Gothel. Sister Miriam Gothel, the administrator and Mother Superior of the Mission of Hope Home for Wayward and Unwanted Children, located on one hundred acres of privately owned forested land twenty miles northwest of Clear Butte.

He could find little else on the facility, except that it had once been owned and operated by the church as a foster care facility for orphaned and abandoned children until it was purchased by an undisclosed corporation.

The gates opened, their hinges squealing with displeasure.

Locke eased his car through the opening, unease dancing up and down his spine.

The home, an early twentieth-century four-story Victorian Gothic castle, loomed at the edge of a densely wooded area in the center of the property, its imposing, statuesque spires clawing at the clouded sky.

Locke stopped his car at the base of the front entry and stared. The mansion glared back, exuding an oppressive weight of history, sorrow, and something far darker.

A middle-aged woman, in her late forties or early fifties, dressed in a stark black nun's habit, greeted him with a silent, unwelcoming grimace as he climbed the cracked concrete steps.

Locke offered his hand in greeting. "Detective Locke," he said.

She glared as if he were leprous, turned and led him through the black, wrought iron and weather-worn oak doors into a cavernous entrance hall. A massive chandelier hung like a skeletal spider from the high arched ceiling, waiting for prey to wander into its web. Polished black-and-white checkered marble tiles, cracked and stained with age, spread like a sea across the ground floor. Faded portraits lined the walls.

A grand staircase spiraled upward from the center of the room, its balustrades carved with twisting vines and strange, human-like faces hidden in the curls of the woodwork.

A suffocating sense of dread saturated the hall, the air thick with forgotten sorrow, weighing Locke down. He stumbled, regained his balance as his scowling guide led him into an expansive library. Shelves lined the walls, climbed from the floor to the high ceiling, groaning beneath the weight of too many books.

"The Abbess will see you in a moment."

The nun closed the doors behind her, left Locke standing and gaping.

He wandered among the nearby stacks, frowning, unable to decipher the worn and faded titles scrawled on the aged and tattered book cover spines. Orderly lines of brownish white stained rectangular tables marched across the center of the room. Eight matching chairs, four to a side, tentatively hugged the tables, uncertain of the affection given or received.

A dainty lounging area loitered near the library entrance. Three diminutive light tan leather settees circled a small circular glass covered table knelt in the center of the settees, supported by four ornately carved legs that disturbingly resembled the humanlike faces carved into the staircase balustrades dominating the main hall.

A throne-like leather armchair plugged the gap between two of the settees nearest the library doors.

Locke noticed that the floor beneath the chair was raised a few inches. He snorted, gazed at the library walls where they snugged the arching ceiling.

Long, rectangular windows filled with a thickly flowing glass and trimmed in a grayish metal, lined the upper portions of the walls. Muddied sunlight filtered through the turbid and grunge-stained glass, fell haphazardly across the polished black-and-white marble tiled floor.

Locke shivered.

The doors opened.

"Detective Locke?"

He turned, masked the sudden disquiet poking his thoughts with a pointy stick. "Mother Gothel?" The epithet he suspected might give him an unguarded reaction.

She twitched a humorless smile, motioned for him to sit in one of the nearby settees. "An affectation bestowed upon me by my children," she said as she glided into the chair on the other side of the table, allowing her to look down on him. "You may call me Sister Miriam."

"Your children?" Locke asked, ignoring her deflection, his tone subtly challenging.

Malice glimmered from her eyes, hugged her age-eroded face. Locke wondered if there might have been beauty there once. Or compassion.

"You must excuse my unintentional possessiveness," she said. "The children that we harbor within our walls have no home, no family, no one they can call mother or father. So of course, they are 'my children.'"

That damned smile again, daring him to contradict her.

The mummified nun who greeted him at the door entered, pushing a silver cart laden with an unadorned white ceramic tea pot, matching cups and small rectangular sandwiches, the crusts shaved off, their pristine white scalps smooth and hairless.

Unlike Olivia's or Rosalinde's shaved heads.

"Tea?" Sister Miriam arched a manicured silver-gray brow.

Locke nodded.

Silence surrounded them as the nun poured the tea and served them.

As the door clicked closed, Sister Miriam asked, "How can I help you, Detective?"

Ignoring his tea and sandwiches, Locke drew a photo from the file folder he brought with him, slid it across the table toward her. "Have you ever seen this boy?" he asked. "Was he ever, one of 'your children?'"

Sister Miriam glanced at the photo, sipped her tea. "I do not believe I have ever seen this boy," she said. "Should I have?"

"Look again," Locke said.

"My memory for faces is excellent, Detective. I know the face and the name of every one of the fifty children currently residing at our home. And I vividly remember the same for every child our home has assisted through the years. I have never seen this boy before." She slid the photo back toward him.

"Have you ever heard the name, Eric Homestead?" Locke said.

Sister Miriam pursed her lips. She shook her head. "The name is not familiar. May I ask what this is about?"

Locke studied her. "How long has the home operated?"

A quiet sigh. She set her tea down, folded spindly and wrinkled hands in her lap. "I believe the home has been here for nearly a century," she said. "It was established by the church in an effort to aid in the care and placement of orphaned and unwanted children into loving and caring families."

Locke eyed a sandwich. A fly crept over the seam of the filling between bread slices. It seemed to test it, shivered, staggered into the air on unstable wings.

"If the home has been here for almost a hundred years, why has no one ever heard of it? Wouldn't the church welcome community involvement in such a noble mission?"

That damned smile, as if he were an insolent child needing maternal correction. "Anonymity has always been the Christian virtue, Detective. And if the community were as benevolent and loving as you naively believe, our home would not be needed."

Her stinging rebuke stabbed his veiled accusation through the heart.

Locke took a moment to gather his trampled thoughts, slid the photo of Eric Homestead into his manila folder. "Who owns the property now?"

"Why, I do," Sister Miriam said. "I purchased it and the home from the church about fifty years ago."

"How old are you?" Where did that come from?

A genuine smile graced Sister Miriam's withered face. Feigned indignation glittered from her eyes. "Why Detective Locke," she said. "In certain polite societal circles, such a bold question to a woman of any age would be considered an offense. I am almost inclined to name a champion to challenge you to a duel to reclaim my besmirched honor." She winked at him.

"Now," she said, "I have numerous duties which I have postponed so that I may entertain your visit. Why are you here?"

"Tell me about Rosalinde Grimm," he said.

"Ah." She lifted a dismissive hand. "The young girl accused of murdering her grandparents. Perhaps she and the young man you are searching for conspired together to commit that heinous crime."

"Rosalinde claims that you imprisoned her here, that you murdered her grandparents and Eric Homestead, and that you stole her unborn twins from her womb."

"Indeed. Quite the melodrama."

"Yes, it is," Locke said.

"Obviously, the girl is distraught over her guilt and is looking to clear her conscience by blaming someone else for her crimes." The Sister arched her brow. "Will there be anything else, Detective?"

"If the community at large is unaware of you or your home, how did Rosalinde Grimm know your name?"

"Please, Detective, you insult my intelligence. We've housed and placed hundreds of children through the decades. Even though we discourage it, people talk." She stood. "My apologies, but I must return to my duties."

Locke stood. "Would you mind if I explored the home and the grounds?"

"I would." The library doors opened. "Unless you have a warrant."

Locke met her stare, shook his head. "I do not."

"I thought not." Sister Miriam motioned to the nun standing in the doorway. "I wish you better luck on your next fishing expedition."

The flash of a curt, emotionless smile. "Sister Rebecca will see you out. Good day, Detective."

The Hag

Sacred Heart Psychiatric Hospital. Fort Collins, Colorado.

The name of my prison for nearly a decade inscribed on the jacket of the guard dumping me into the common room, what we inmates called the Crazy Room. My reward for choosing to speak with my new doctor, a haggard and exhausted woman in her late forties, who looked like she wished to be anywhere else than here more than I did.

I stared at my attendant's name tag as a sly hand slid from my breast and down my side, lingered on my butt, fingers cupping my flesh. He leered and winked, turned and shoved me through the double doors into restless chaos.

Gary. Our daytime floor nurse. Perhaps tonight as well. If I framed my invitation correctly.

A new name. A new face. An ancient avarice. Another in a lengthening list of grievances that I would need to shove back into the murky pit of my vengeance. I had other matters to attend to.

I zombie-staggered to the calendar tacked lifelessly to the wall, touched mindless fingers to the date. Nine years and six months since my permanent incarceration. Two months until my babies' birthday. Abigail and Anne. Ten years old. I needed to be back in Clear Butte by then to celebrate their birthing day and to destroy the Heralds of the Seventh Seal. And Mother Gothel.

My time to act grew short. But today, I knew she would be in the Crazy Room. Yasmina Bitterlich. The Hag. At one time, Mother Gothel's right hand. Her name whispered in the halls when Mother Gothel could not hear. No one in the Seventh Seal knew what had caused their division. But in her wrath, Mother Gothel had consigned Yasmina to perpetual imprisonment in Sacred Heart Psychiatric Hospital.

A fossilized lifer. Aside from me, none of the current inmates knew how long she'd been here. But they knew who she was and what she could do if they crossed her. Not even the staff messed with her. But I needed her. I needed her to release the curse sealed away by Mother Gothel the night she stole my children.

The common room was quiet this morning, the usual din of incoherent words and chaotic conversations a mere buzz of a few unhinged bees rather than the normal flood of the inharmonious hive.

Our guards hovered conspicuously near the doors, the corners of the common room, and at the windows. Steel-enhanced mesh entwined the thick, double-paned glass, slicing the streaming sunlight into shadowed, diamond-shaped cuts, jumbling it like the pieces of a puzzle.

An aged black-and-white sitcom stumbled from the television clamped to the wall above the game cabinet. Worn out, disintegrating boxes lined the cabinet shelves, their gleaming cardboard images faded and forgotten, the games they imprisoned saddened references to normal times no longer remembered.

The veiled stench of urine and unwashed bodies hung in the stagnant air, clawed paws scratching at the doors to be let out.

Yasmina sat alone in the corner on the far side of the common room. Shadows dappled her wizened face, stroked the long, sinewy tangles of her silver-gray hair, pulling them down over bent shoulders. The twisted ends trembled against her dull off-white hospital gown, tasting the cool, manufactured air like a snake's tongue. She stared blankly into the distance, cloudy eyes empty, the spark of consciousness buried. The shriveled ends of her mouth sagged, stretching desiccated and withered skin like sun-scorched leather. Gnarled hands worried themselves in her emaciated lap, scraggy fingers twitching spider-like, flicking the air sitting upon her thighs.

Discordant voices stumbled through the room, mumbling and muttering, whining and griping, the words floating across the empty spaces, nonsensical and devoid of coherent thought. Gowned bodies trudged and blundered back and forth, shoulders slumped, drugged expressions, the light glowing behind the eyes dimmed and vacuous, minds empty.

I leaned back against the wall, shoulders pressed against the calendar. The double stable-like doors leading into the Crazy Room were locked from the outside. I knew. I tried to open them the first time I was granted the privilege of occupying the room, provoking a litany of verbal rebukes vomited from the surly mouths of our captors. They watched me closely now, tensed, their attention divided between myself and another they had named as an agitator.

It was a label I wore, like a badge of honor. It gave me a purpose other than the madness that brought me here.

My imprisonment chafed. I felt the passage of time as it slipped through my grasping fingers, dismantling my purpose.

Wistful memories flitted through my thoughts; an image of my beloved Eric, the first time I saw him when he came to collect me from my grandparents for the Heralds and Mother Gothel. Our stolen time together during my lengthening captivity, the love that grew between us, despite Mother Gothel's plans to give me to another. Our final, hopeless night, Mother Yasmina's plot to assist our escape discovered, Eric's murder, and my frantic escape after I stabbed Mother Gothel.

I no longer recalled his face. I was forbidden to keep trinkets from my past, though I had managed to hide a single reminder of that nightmare. It drove my purpose to punish those who had taken everything from me with the same suffering with which they had bludgeoned me.

My hand strayed to my shorn hair, the golden red locks hacked off by Mother Gothel in her rage and kept shaven by the minions of the Heralds of the Seventh Seal as a constant reminder of my depravity and failure. Her oath that she would have my children as penance for my sins.

Vengeance sustained me.

I sat carefully next to the old woman. She did not acknowledge my existence. I hesitated, my gaze following the path Gary traversed through the shifting maze of ambling bodies. Our gazes touched for an instant. I smiled blankly at him. He frowned and paused. I recognized the thoughts tumbling through his mind. I quirked a flirtatious smile, raised a brow in invitation.

Carnal intent flitted through his eyes. He returned my smile, a familiar and knowing expression settling upon his chunky face.

Tonight then. He nodded, wandered away, turning his attention to less urgent matters.

The promised activity turned my stomach. But I had to survive if I was to avenge myself upon Mother Gothel and the three Fathers responsible for my torment.

Certain that we were not watched, I reached across the distance and touched the old woman's arm. She flinched, returned to her catatonia. Leaning over, I whispered, "Mother Yasmina."

Eyes blinked.

I pulled in a slow, heavy breath. My heart hammered my chest. "Mother Yasmina," I repeated. "It is I—" I paused. Uncertainty pricked my purpose. I licked dry, trembling lips. "Rosalinde Grimm. You tried once to save me and my unborn children from Mother Gothel's wrath."

Cold shivers danced through her shriveled body. She shook her head, coughed regret from her chest. "It cannot be," she muttered. "Rosalinde Grimm and her children are long dead." Sanity fled. She sagged into her chair.

My hope seeped away. Desperation filled the void. I could not fail.

Studious eyes upon us. I smiled weakly, patted the old woman's ravaged arm, smoothed her gown over an emaciated leg. The eyes continued their examination, turned a heartbeat later to more urgent matters at one of the windows across the room.

I turned her face gently toward me, leaned closer, captured her empty stare. "No," I said. "I am here. It is I, Rosalinde. And I need your aid."

A withered hand reached up, stroked my cheek. Clarity drew back the curtains to light her memories. She smiled, her mouth trembling. "Rosalinde?"

"Yes," I responded, the eagerness in my voice causing me to wince. I needed to practice patience. There would not be a second chance if I lost this opportunity.

Her eyes wandered over my face, slid upward to my head. Her smile faltered, chased from her face by a darkening frown. She touched my shaven scalp, desiccated fingers crawling across the scars.

"Your beautiful hair," she said. "Gone." Sorrow bubbled in her voice.

"Mother Gothel took my hair the night she stole my unborn children," I said.

Her frown deepened. The spark of memories flared.

"Mother Gothel?"

"Yes," I responded, excitement winding up my eagerness like a child's toy. "Mother Gothel took my hair. I need you to give it back to me."

"You're not Rosalinde Grimm." She leaned over, drool leaking from between her parted lips. "Rosalinde would know not to ask for such a thing."

Desperation drove me. I gripped her arm. "Please," I begged. "Mother Gothel took everything from me. She destroyed my life."

Wizened eyes narrowed. "You do not know what you ask, my child."

"I *do* know," I said. "And I am willing to pay the price."

She grinned, madness dripping from her clouded eyes. She touched my scalp. "We shall see," she said, then cackled.

Fairy Tale

RAPUNZEL!

Rapunzel!

Let down your hair!

Then I may claim your golden stair!

Midnight.

The memory of Gary and his greasy hands wandering my body, his gooey lips pressed into mine, his tongue slitting my mouth. His guttural grunting. His body on top of mine. Blessed silence when I slid the blade of my stolen knife into his throat.

I quietly entered Mother Yasmina's room after my midnight delight with Gary, barred the door to ensure privacy.

Lit candles surrounded us. Their flames guttered, threw grotesque and monstrous shadows against the walls. Trails of smoke slithered into the dim air, floated below the dust-darkened ceiling. A tempestuous storm of aromas and fragrances swirled through the room, wheedling and coaxing.

Yasmina slumped in a plastic armchair, her eyes burning sulfur yellow and crimson. Her quivering lips chanted the silent call, invoking the demons and their curse. I sat across from her, my plastic armchair creaking as I rocked in my seat. Invisible claws scraped the tiled floor outside our circle of protection, dug slender gouges into the laminate.

I shivered, foreboding and dread dancing down my spine.

Thunder cracked. Lightning sparked.

My skull split open like a crushed pecan shell.

Voices slithered in the dark, scratching and scraping the inside of my head. Pain throbbed. Lightning blazed, struck the ground of my mind, splintering thoughts into needle-like fragments.

I bit through my lower lip, stifled the scream boiling up from the pit of my chest. It shuddered and trembled, nearly pulverized the last of my will.

"Make it stop," I cried. "Please."

Yasmina sat across from me in her sagging plastic chair, the arms cracked and cleaved. Dark, moldy slivers scored the shriveled flesh of her wizened arms. She glared at me and grinned, her mouth an empty black hole that pulled me forward and downward into the abyss.

She cackled. "Too late. Too late to stop. Too late to cage the beast, once released."

She leered at me, her pitch-dark eyes glinting with malevolent power.

I shivered. My hands balled into fists, nails digging furrows into my palms. Raw pain seared my flesh. My arms jerked, pulled against the leather tethers binding my wrists to the chair arms. My legs kicked, jerking the chair legs. Plastic grated against the laminate. The chair bounced and skipped.

The door latch rattled, but the lock wouldn't turn. I made sure of that. A muffled voice from outside. An urgent tone that climbed to rising panic. Fists pounded on the door. The heavy thump of a body followed.

A faint moan floated into the air. Mine. Lights flashed and danced before my eyes. The voices grew. Urgency pushed me forward. I resisted. Hands grasped at my thoughts, my sanity. They pulled me from the light and down into the pitch-black gloom.

My shaved and scarred scalp itched and tingled, a universe of needles jabbing through my skin. Blood oozed. The voices clamored, chanted and crooned, the rhyme dripping from invisible lips. Words splashed like acid at the crumbling foundations of my soul. Shimmering golden red hair sprouted and grew, yearned toward the emptiness surrounding me, grew thicker and stronger. The strands began to writhe and twist to a soundless melody. Agony wrenched my body. Leather dug into my wrists and ankles.

I jerked and twitched. Hair coiled, thrashed the air, tips stabbing the shadows. Malevolent laughter echoed through my mind, rattled against my skull.

The pounding against the door increased. A muffled chorus of panicked voices seeped through, tumbled to the floor just beyond the threshold. The lock jiggled, slowly turned.

Yasmina screeched. Her wrinkled and furrowed face loomed closer. Her eyes burned with fire. An earthen jar appeared in her trembling, translucent hands. Veins bulged against the paper-thin flesh, pulsing with crimson. The ancient symbol etched into the clay glowed. Malevolence throbbed between us, hammered my thoughts.

"Remember your purpose," she whispered. "Remember your loss. Remember your grief. Remember your rage. Remember your vengeance."

I licked dry lips, swallowed past a parched throat. The jar drew me closer, reached for and snagged my thoughts. Blinding light burned away the veil. Memories flooded past. My soul twisted and knotted, warping the strands springing from my head.

Outrage blossomed, flooded my consciousness.

I screamed, the sound ripping from my chest.

Yasmina shoved the jar at me. "You must say the words," she said. The lid bounced, settled, bubbled around the brim. "Say the words!"

My head snapped back as if slapped. I licked blood from my bottom lip, leaned forward, and stared into the venom glaring up at me from the oblivion. I opened my mouth, croaked the first word. "Rapunzel."

The lid jumped, settled, continued to boil.

My mouth was a desert. I choked out the next word. "Rapunzel."

The jar top bounced and rolled over the rim.

"Complete the rhyme!"

My body spasmed. I arched my back, shoved my heart into my ribs. Agony erupted. The final words spewed from my parched throat. "Let down your hair! Then I may claim your golden stair!"

The lid blew off the jar. Desolation followed. Emptiness grasped me, choked and strangled. Something stared out through my eyes as my hair exploded, engulfing Yasmina in a golden red firestorm.

She screamed and shrieked, cocooned in a writhing mass of knots and braids. She slumped in her chair, a single bulging, bloodshot eye glaring out from the twitching brambles and barbs.

My hair consumed me, shattered my mind. I thrashed and flailed. My chair fell over. My head bounced off the floor, spiked my thoughts with pitch-dark evil.

The door to Yasmina's room flew open, slammed against the wall.

My heart stuttered and died.

A Friendly Face

BRIGHT, COLORLESS SUNLIGHT CHEWS away the shadows clinging to me and the park bench.

Gravel crunches beneath the pounding beat of approaching footfalls. Pebbles skid past, kicking up diminutive dust tornadoes. A tall, lanky shadow drapes across me, blotting out the glowing daylight.

"Are you okay? Do you need some help?" A man's voice, dripping with concern.

Tap. Tap. Tap. Tap.

Leaves slap against swaying tree branches, their unending snickers thumping the back of my head.

I shudder. Trembling fingers caress the lonely silver satin stiletto on the seat beside me, smearing crimson across cracked wood as I drag my hands into my lap, square my body with the bench seat, demurely pull my legs beneath the bench, ankles crossed. My toes clench the damp grass as I swallow down the sand, scratching the back of my throat. A voice whispers in my mind, dredging up the rhyme and the words from the pit where it hunkers, leering from the dark.

Rapunzel!

Rapunzel!

"Stop."

"Stop what? I'm not—"

I look up, mouth pinching into a tight line, and shake my head. *Please go away.*

A man stands before me on the path, feet clothed in luxury, slender legs and hips embraced by yoga leggings, a lean torso draped with a gauzy muscle shirt. Sinew and muscle strain underneath sun-kissed flesh. He stares, eyes narrowing, expression knotting with worry.

I heave a breath. *Eric?*

He holds out his phone. "Hey, I'm sorry if I startled you. I didn't mean…I'm not trying to…you know." His words trail into an anxious silence, thrashing and twitching at his feet like a dying fish. "You look like you could use some help. Can I call someone? The police? An ambulance?"

Not my beloved. But enough like him to wring my heart like a soaked cloth.

You can call anyone you like. Just not for me.

"No," I say. "I'm not distressed. But thank you for your kind offer. I appreciate your concern."

Doubt crawls through his eyes. "Are you sure? I mean…you look like crap."

I tug the shadow of a smile. And how should a lady take your vulgar comment regarding her appearance?

"Please," I say. "There is no need for your worry. Truly, it was a difficult evening. But I have recovered now and was enjoying my morning before you interrupted me."

A dubious expression darts across his face. Worry creases his brow. He examines me, appraising, purses his lips, indecision poking his visage. "Don't take this the wrong way," he says. "But you look like a wood chipper vomited you out." Hesitation. He chews his lower lip, not unlike Eric's endearing habit when vexed.

Sudden fondness plucks a shy smile. I divert my gaze, unable to decide if I want this stranger to leave me alone in my guilt and grief or if I would rather enjoy his company. I wonder if his touch would be as gentle as my beloved's. His caress as soothing. His lips as delectable.

He clears his throat. "And you were talking to yourself."

I look up.

"The conversation sounded pretty intense. Are you sure you don't need some help?" He gestures toward a building across the street from the park. "My church is just over there."

I follow his gaze, stare at the red brick and white paneled building squatting in the middle of the block, the tarnished white clapboard steeple adorning the roof crown, note the faded white wood and red brick sign jutting from a narrow concrete curb slicing the two-lane entrance to the parking lot.

My stomach sours.

The voices hiss and sigh, enticing and cajoling. My mind tilts, slides closer to the edge of the abyss. A name is muttered.

Rapunzel!

I shake my head.

It itches beneath my hat, my scalp throbbing, honey-gold needles thrusting through the soil of my flesh.

"I'm sorry," he says, pushes his hand at me. "Thomas Eldridge."

I gawk at his extended hand. A deer in the headlights.

His hand remains for an uncomfortable moment before retreating to a more respectful distance.

Rapunzel!

"Are you a priest of the Seventh Seal?"

An awkward silence.

"The seventh what?" He shakes his head. "I'm not familiar with that, uh...denomination."

"Please leave me alone."

He holds up his hands in mock self-defense. "If you're worried that I'm Catholic or Protestant, I'm not. And I'm not a priest. Of any kind."

My eyes meet his.

The voices continue to rumble inside my thoughts.

Let down your hair!

Writhing strands fill my hat.

"I'm actually just a pastor. We're nondenominational."

"Not the Heralds of the Seventh Seal?"

He frowns, shakes his head. "I don't even know what that is."

"Not part of the Church?"

"The Catholic Church? Uh, no. As I said."

He presents his hand once more, open and inviting.

"I don't know what kind of trouble you're in, but I can help." Silence. His eyes widen. An entreaty.

So then I may—

"No!"

He staggers back, surprise and fear creasing his face.

I snatch my sandal from beside me, hug it to my chest as I stand. My hair squirms and flails under my hat, the ends poking through the sides. Torment stabs my heart. Distress winds crushing fingers around my shredded soul.

"I must go," I say. "I...I have an appointment."

Before he can respond, I stagger away, stumble down the gravel path, kicking grit, sand, and pebbles, spewing dust in my wake, my thoughts heavy with grief and memories of the man Thomas Eldridge reminds me of.

Rapunzel

DETECTIVE LOCKE

Detective William Locke trudges up white-washed concrete steps, pulling him into the open and waiting maw of Saint Thomas Aquinas parish. Despite the warm mid-morning late spring breeze tickling the back of his neck, he shivers, the chill grip of an icy fist squeezing his heart. A pair of crows stare down at him from their perch at the edge of the roof, their depthless black eyes watching, piercing the armor he's erected to guard his darkest thoughts and emotions.

Muted conversation dies as he breaches the porch. Eyes stare, tracing his steps as he plods across the pitted concrete and pauses at the open doors. Ten-year-old memories of his wife, Olivia, and their children in their upstairs bathroom, water streaming over the lip of the tub, flooding the bathroom floor, mixing with the blood flowing from the back of Olivia's head, soaking the hallway carpet, and oozing down the stairs.

He'd held their funerals here, had endured the priest's incessant attempts to console him and ensure him that his children were with God. Not Oliva. Just the children.

He'd never punched a priest before.

Locke clears his throat, wrenches his eyes away from the dimmed light embracing the doorway, the terror-stuffed memories seeping through the chinks in his tarnished and rusted armor.

Images prance past, digging and scraping, chipping away flakes from his corroded defenses. They flutter to his feet, scattered by the wheezing wind.

Water streamed down the stairs from the second floor of their faux two-story Victorian; his and Olivia's dream home, purchased after he had been promoted to detective. The water pooled at the base of the stairs, soaked the carpet in a slowly expanding oval sea.

"Olivia?" Silence, except for the gurgling murmur of the water flowing down the stair steps, and the indistinct sputter and splash of running water from the top of the stairs.

Alarmed, Locke bounded up the steps, took two or three at a time, drew his service weapon as he called his wife's name again.

He discovered them in the bathroom.

Jacob and Deborah, three and five, his pride and joy, bobbing face down in a sea of soapy bubbles as water brimmed over the bathtub lip. Olivia slumped against the wall, eyes vacant, staring at the blood splattering the ceiling, her head shaved, a revolver clutched in her hand, crimson-shaded water soaking her nightgown.

He slammed his knees into the porcelain floor tiles, reached out with shaking fingers. They hovered, unable to touch the water-logged heads, his body twisted into knots.

The investigation and its conclusion, murder-suicide stemming from chronic postpartum depression, despite his insistence that his wife and children were the victims of something far more insidious and malevolent. That his wife's fears were not some simple psychoses but were fed by a growing dread of an unknown power that terrified her.

No evidence of a break-in. No evidence of an intruder or intruders. No evidence of an unknown or hidden group stalking Locke's family. Just the open book of *The Original Folk and Fairy Tales of the Brothers*

Grimm he found on their bed, the story of Rapunzel glowering up at him, notes in Olivia's handwriting scrawled in the margins and between the lines. He later found the receipt for the book shoved inside a journal she kept. A journal he didn't know about. A journal detailing Olivia's growing obsession with the story of Rapunzel and her unnaturally long and flowing hair. Why Olivia feared to allow her own hair to grow out long and her obsession with the length of Deborah's hair.

The squeal of brakes shakes Locke from the prison of his memories. He blinks and turns toward the police barricades spanning the parking lot below. A crowd gathers. Curious neighborhood locals. The ghoulish. People fascinated by death, hopeful in their desire to gaze upon a mangled corpse.

The media. His worst nightmare. He whispers a profanity that Olivia would have scolded him for uttering.

The crows squawk, their discordant, screeching cackles skipping goose bumps down his back. They flap from their roof roost into the sky, the thwack of their wings rattling the back of his skull.

Swallowing down the dread clogging his throat, Locke motions to a nearby patrolman. The officer hesitates, his eyes begging those beside him to rescue him from Detective Death's summons. They ignore him, hiding behind poorly disguised trepidation, forcing the man to respond to Locke's beckoning. Locke studies the officer in silence. It's been ten years since Olivia murdered their children then committed suicide. Ten years for the stench of death clinging to him to fade. And still, the memory of that day trails him as if it happened yesterday.

"Detective?"

Locke notices the quiver in the man's voice, tries to guess the patrolman's age, sifts through fractured memories for a name to pin to the strained expression and the anxious eyes refusing to meet his own.

The whiff of a memory. His stomach sours. Henry Johnson. Of course. Words spoken by Locke's granddad about his military experiences in World War II roll in on tentative waves; 'loose lips sink ships.' Johnson's girlfriend is a reporter, probably standing in the crowd of looky-loos straining for their fifteen seconds of fame. Still, better to keep the gossip close and know who to shish kabob when their investigation goes south.

Johnson nods, clears the hairball from his throat, deer-like terror prancing across his face.

Locke pulls him close. "I want you on crowd control. No one gets past the barricades. *Especially* the media." He pauses, making sure Johnson understands the implied threat in his voice. "Got it?"

Johnson flicks a glance at the expanding crowd, nods again, his Adam's apple jerking.

Snorting, Locke brushes past him, steps through the veil dividing the world of the living from the nightmare of the dead.

Death assaults him.

He hesitates, coughs up the stench from his lungs, clenching his notebook to his side to steady his fraying nerves. Why did it have to be a church? Especially this one?

Unsteady sunlight slices through the shadowed gloom, spears the center isle with jaundiced bile. Crime scene tape drapes over the sharply angled arms of the orderly pews, marking the edges of an obscene and straight-arrowed yellow brick road that leads to a crucified Wizard of Oz.

Locke halts his unwilling journey at the base of the altar, looks up at the grizzly scene. His gut lurches.

"Locke." Keith Fox, his partner. The only detective on the force that will work with him.

Locke nods, wipes his mouth with the back of his hand, opens his notebook. "Got an I.D.?" Stupid question. He already knows the answer.

Silence. The rustle of paper.

"Preliminary. Father Augustus Matthews. The parish priest."

Locke peers and gestures. "Is that rope tying the body to the crucifix?"

"Not rope. Hair. Lots and lots of hair."

Locke shivers. Memories not quite grasped slide past and vanish. "And the flowers shoved into his mouth?"

A shrug. "Not local. Working on identifying them."

"They're Rapunzel." A crime scene technician stands beside him, peering up at the grizzly scene.

"What?"

"Sorry." The technician points at the flowers. "Rapunzel. More commonly known as bellflower."

Locke frowns.

"My grandmother grew them here in a greenhouse. She liked to garden." He gestures at the sigil carved into the center of the priest's chest. "Same flower that's in the center of that."

Locke studies the bloody emblem: a seven-petaled bellflower in the center of a ring of seven thorny brambles connected by bloody threads, also dripping blood. He turns away from the priest's body, a vision of the ropes of crimson-stained hair tying it to the crucifix, the white, violet-tipped flowers drooping from the sagging open jaw. He shudders, his wife's pleading voice tapping his shoulder.

Bless Me, Father

THE STEEPLE BELLS OF Our Blessed Mother parish chime twelve noon, vibrating the bones of the church with each baritone ring.

I pause at the entrance to the nave beside the bowl of holy water, staring into its liquid depths, at my rippling reflection. I touch the surface after a brief hesitation, bring my fingers toward my face and body. They falter, water dripping from their tips. My thoughts wander. Memories flash past, teasing and seductive.

Meandering through a Fort Collins city park at dusk, wrapped in reminiscences of my beloved and the twin daughters we created together, who slumbered in my swollen womb. The unanticipated appearance of Mother Gothel with Father Confessor Sebastian Oldham. The murder of an innocent bystander who happened upon my plight. My abduction and imprisonment.

I shudder, wipe my hands down the sides of the filmy blue pastel blouse and mid-thigh box pleated skirt I stole from the sorting bins behind a nearby thrift store, swipe away a stray tear trying to roll down my cheek. My hand finds the folded linen cloth inside my waistband holding the withering stem and wilting petals of Rapunzel I have brought.

I stand just outside the entrance to the auditorium and wait, my heart thudding. Inside, two or three of the faithful and penitent linger, faces turned toward the altar and the priest as he finishes his message.

A collective sigh shivers the air. Fabric scrapes and chafes the pew seats, accompanied by whispered conversation and the click of hard-soled shoes on the ceramic floor tiles. Bodies brush past me, faces averted except for one who pins me with a curious stare.

I look away, hide my face with my hand, suddenly ashamed, but not understanding why.

The gentle click of the closing doors pulls my attention from my chagrin.

"May I help you?"

I suck a gasp and blink.

Rapunzel!

Father Confessor Sebastian Oldham stands before me, older, grayer, body thicker, hair thinner. But I recognize him. His face scored into my memory with fire and blood. He is perhaps in his late fifties, square face and chin, silvered brown hair and flinty brown eyes. He studies me, hands clasped at his waist, his parochial robes hanging limp from a once athletic body beginning to plump like a fattened calf.

I force a nervous smile, allow guilt to skim across my face. My cheeks heat as I press my hands against the false elfin bulge of my stomach. "Father Sebastian Oldham?" I ask shyly.

His eyes narrow, glide downward, hesitate for a heartbeat. "Do I know you?"

I shake my head. "No, Father. We have never met."

"Then how—"

"A former parishioner. We were friends in Fort Collins. She told me to come see you when I arrived in Clear Butte." I lower my gaze in spurious shame and contrition. "I have come for confession."

A calculated lull. "How far along are you?"

I pause, listen for the voices muttering in the back of my mind. Hissing murmurs rise from the depths and wind suffocating vines around my soul. Base and vile words pour outward. Sharpened steel scrapes the inside of my skull. Shivers dance over my body.

Concern wipes away judgment. "Are you alright, my dear? Can I—"

I swat away his empathy. "I am fine, Father," I say. "The emotions—"

He nods. "Does your husband know you are here?"

"I...am not married."

"Ah. Are you a member of the Church?"

"I am." The words spoken too quickly, too desperately.

Uneasy quiet.

He narrows his eyes. My tone has pricked his memories, his struggle to tease out the correct one.

I touch his arm. "Father, please," I say. "I am new here and weighed down with the guilt of my sin." I press my hands against my stomach. "I...we have no one else."

Rapunzel!

The memory he reaches for dissolves like the morning mist. His expression relaxes.

"Your friend didn't accompany you?"

Humiliation flashes. "I...did not know his name. We were together for only a night." I lower my eyes, chew my bottom lip, force the false tears from my eyes. "I was—"

He touches my shoulder, guides me to the back of the nave and the confessional. "Please, no more, my child. Not out here." He opens the door for me, enters the other side.

I sit in solitude, my thoughts squirming, my scalp burning with acid as my red gold locks worm their way up through the soil of my skull. The voices stroke my mind, their festering, leprous touch blistering my consciousness with boils and gangrenous sores.

Let down your hair!

I shudder, close my eyes, biting through the inside of my cheek to press down the shrieks beginning to boil in the pit of my soul. My hat topples from my head. I catch it, chew the brim, tears bubbling from my eyes, the taloned ends of my hair quietly scraping the walls of the confessional.

The grille door slides open. I hear the priest's raspy breathing, smell the sweat gathering upon his forehead, the odor of his breath and the remnants of his breakfast. Memories chase through my crumbling thoughts, tugged into the morass of madness by the chorus of wheezing voices and their discordant litany.

My resolve slowly crumbles beneath the crushing weight of my writhing hair and its tangles of brambles.

Until the priest speaks, and memories of agony and rage char my guilt to ash.

"My dear child," he says. "Are you there?" Apprehension, accompanied by the silken scrape of cloth across flesh.

Then I may claim your golden stair!

I collapse against the booth wall, press my face to the latticed grille, embracing the blanketing darkness. "Bless you, Father," I say. "For you have greatly sinned." I lick my lips, suck desiccated air down my throat, torturous ecstasy searing my mind. "And you have never confessed your sin."

A sudden intake of air. "What?"

I scream. My hair blasts through the grille, shattering wood, tossing spear-tipped splinters into the air above. The priest cries out, struggles against the thickening vines as they wrap and squeeze his body, snapping bone, wrenching joints apart.

The confessional explodes, vomits splinters through the surrounding spaces.

I fling him from the shattered remnants of the booth. His body crashes into a front pew, flops to the floor. I follow, my hair twisting and turning, the ends snaking over crimson-smeared wood. He stares, his chest sputtering, terror leaking from his bulging eyes. One arm lies twisted and broken; the shoulder wrenched from the socket. A leg twitches at unnatural angles. Blood soaks his cassock, puddling on the floor beneath him.

A hand reaches up, snags the leg of the pew. He drags his fractured body a few tormented inches before I catch him, drag him back to the remains of the confessional booth, slam him into the rubble of the penitent side. His chest heaves, struggling to find the breath leaking from the hole piercing his side.

I lean down, drag the backs of my fingers down his blood-slimed cheek, my hair floating above us, dripping crimson. The voices chatter with impatience, eager for their next meal.

I twitch a smile. "Bless me, Father, for I have sinned." I giggle, the madness on my shoulder nestling against my neck, cooing a comforting song. "It has been less than five minutes since my last confession." I graze my lips against his ear. "I'm not pregnant. But I was. Once. You were there, in the park, the night she came for me. You killed an innocent."

I lean back. "I would offer you confession for your unrepentant sins...but I am not a priest. And I do not care that your blackened soul shall rot in hell."

His eyes widen with recognition, the memory now fully exposed. His chest sputters, blood bubbling from his parted lips. He shakes his head. "No."

"Yes." I straddle him, tuck the single stem of violet-streaked Rapunzel into the collar of his vestment robes, lean down upon his shoulders. "Where are my children?" I ask. "The ones you sold to Mother Gothel for thirty pieces of silver?"

He shakes his head. "I cannot—" blood bubbles from between quivering lips, choking the words tumbling from his mouth. "She will—"

The shrill screech of a child's scream shatters our quiet conversation.

I stumble from the debris, into the aisle.

A withered crone dressed in a black high-collared, ankle-length, long-sleeved dress stands in the center of the aisle, long flowing silver-stained braids coiled chastely about her narrow head. In each veined and shriveled fist she grasps the hand of an identical young girl, each adorned with pixie-cut golden red hair and emerald eyes framed in an oval face and rounded chin.

The girl on my left gapes. Her youthful face twists in terror. The other on my right scowls, rage flashing from her emerald eyes, her childish expression warping with outrage and vehemence. Both girls wear my face. My beloved Eric's face.

I stagger to an uncertain stop. My heart lurches in my chest, thuds against my ribs. My breath deserts me, and I falter to a knee. A trembling hand clutches the knobbed end of the back of a pew. My twitching and writhing locks shrink and fall limp, their splintered and fractured ends bursting into sparking flames. Red gold ashes flutter to my feet, stain the floor a deep purplish red. My gut contorts and coils. My heart thunders.

"Harlot."

The word bludgeons my cheek. My head snaps to the side.

My gaze pivots to the old woman. "Witch," I hiss and stand, the voices scraping my thoughts with ragged bone. My splintered and gnarled locks thrash the air. Wretched torment lacerates my skull. I step toward them, the first word of my litany dripping with gore from my mouth.

Rapunzel!

Mother Gothel straightens, her chin lifted in defiance and cold, calculating malice, her eyes blazing. "You would slay me now, in front of the children? Your children?"

Gasps.

"Mama?"

The girl on my left. Anna, the voices whisper in my mind. Her cropped hair convulses and shudders for an instant.

The girl on my right disentangles her hand from Mother's Gothel's clawed paw, steps in front of her. Abigail, her expression ferocious and savage. She clenches her fists in a fighter's stance, her body tensed and whiplike, prepared to strike. A miniature she-bear defending the mama bear.

My daughters, whom I do not know, who do not know me.

My heart sputters for a beat. My rage melts, and I collapse to the floor, my squirming and slithering locks falling lifeless about my shoulders, chest, and back. I reach out with a shaking hand. Tears streak my face. My lips twist with grief and heart-rending loss.

Mother Gothel smirks. "This is the disciple of which I have spoken," she says. "A harlot and a murderer. Possessed by demons. Her mind twisted by jealousy and rage until it snapped. Now do you understand why I have never allowed you to know her?"

Abigail steps toward me, her outrage kicking me in the gut. She glances at the human detritus scattered behind me. She spits at me. "You will pay for what you have done," she says, her child's voice piercing my jagged thoughts.

My gaze slides to Anna. She stands rigid, confusion and uncertainty warring across her face, her eyes flicking back-and-forth from me to

Mother Gothel and back. The anguish tormenting her soul flutters behind her eyes, is yanked into the shadows by the demon skulking within the depths of her innocent soul.

"Mama?" Anna whispers, the question directed toward me and not Mother Gothel. She lifts a tentative hand.

Mother Gothel steps forward, shoves the girls behind her. She yanks a phone from her clutch, dials 9-1-1, her dark and dangerous eyes glittering with malevolence. "Yes," she says. "I need to report a murder."

The demons clamor for her blood and her soul. But I cannot claim either in the moment. Not in front of my daughters. As the voices tear and rend what remains of my soul, I blunder to my feet and flee through the back of the church.

Fallen Angel

I HOVER JUST INSIDE the line of meandering trees dotting Mirror Lake Park. A thin veil of tattered white clouds obscure the late afternoon sun, chasing faint shadows across the manicured lawn and pink gravel paths. Across the vacant street squats a red brick and white-washed sided building. A matching sign hunkers down upon a cracked concrete curb splitting the dingy gray asphalt parking lot.

Clear Butte Community Church.

Pastor Thomas Eldridge.

The name feels familiar. I taste the letters on the tip of my tongue. A recent memory floats to the surface. A lean, smiling face, sandy blond hair, and kind, inviting blue eyes. The right hand of fellowship held out to me. An offer of aid.

Refused.

I had an appointment with a priest.

Blood drenches my blouse and skirt, smears my face, hands and arms, coats my trembling legs. The street is deserted. The park vacant. My walk is not far. I should not, however. This man who reminds me of my beloved Eric deserves better than what I am about to give him. But his invitation pulls me forward.

I stroll across the open lawn, arms crossed, slide behind an unlit lamp post as a car drives past. I remain unseen and undiscovered. After jogging across the empty street, I slip behind the church building, jimmy open a window and climb through.

I collapse into the shadowed corner of a small office. Acid abrades my skull, strips away the layers of my sanity, exposing depravity and wickedness underneath. Ashes swirl in miniature tornadoes, riven by the wind of evil crouching in the deepest recesses of my mind.

I hug my knees to my chest. The remnants of my hair flutter to the floor around me, the singed strands cork screwing, glowing orange, before crumbling into cinders that twist about for a breath and vanish.

The chorus of demons, satiated from their last meal, lie dormant, cuddling together at the fractured doorway to my warped and perverted soul.

The open window breathes warm air into the confining space. Sharp, piercing caws of crows ride the crawling breeze, shattering the fragile quiet embracing me.

Sanguine tears streak my face.

A haunted memory loops through my thoughts. The high-pitched screams of two young girls holding hands with the witch. The horror etched into their faces. Fierce Abigail, her mind beginning to be twisted by the malevolence and greed of Mother Gothel, but her soul unsullied by the demons or their curse. She is the younger. Sheepish Anna. Apprehensive and reluctant. Uncertain. The demons peek from her blackening soul, whisper to her through her thoughts and in her dreams. Despite Mother Gothel's attempts, she does not believe what she has been told. She and I are true soulmates, sharing the demons and the curse. She is the older.

Mein Liebling.

I snuffle, wipe away the snot seeping out from my nose. "Go away."

I cannot.

"You're dead."

And yet I am here. With the demons.

The sobs convulse my body. The breath catches in my throat.

Why are you crying?

"Why do you care?"

You are my child. My Rosalinde.

A bitter smile creases my lips. "Rosalinde is dead. I am Rapunzel."

I know.

"Then why?"

A quiet, bitter chuckle. You are not the first to lose what you held most dearly in your heart to Mother Gothel.

The door opens. Light spills through the sudden void, embracing a tall, lean shadow, face cloaked in ink. The figure crosses the threshold, though a hesitant hand remains wrapped around the latch. The other clutches a baseball bat.

"Who's there?"

A familiar voice.

The figure in the doorway raises the baseball bat. "I don't want any trouble. If you want money, I have a little."

I reach out with a shaking hand. "Eric? My beloved?"

The baseball bat clatters to the floor.

A man kneels beside me. Smooth, lean face, oval chin, kind eyes overflowing with worry and concern. Recognition flares, lips purse.

"What the hell?"

He skims his hands over me, pulls them away, shaking, smeared with blood. Not mine. I do not think.

"Where did you come from? How did you—?" His eyes slide to the broken window, skate down, settle upon my face. "I really need to get some decent locks. Come on."

He pulls me from my corner, drapes my body across muscular arms that tremble with exertion. A laborious journey into a bedroom where I am gently placed upon a bed. Eyes stare down, wrapped in compassion and empathy, pursued by fretful unease.

"What have you gotten yourself into?"

"Eric?" I reach into the distance, fingers stretching into infinity. "Have you come back for me?" My hand falls.

Eric's face blurs and fades.

I awaken to the silken touch of a warm, moist cloth upon my face. It glides down my cheeks, over my neck, across my forehead. My eyes flutter open. Eric? A familiar face leans over me, frowning with concentration, his tender caresses smoothing away the anguish and unease. Not Eric. Then who?

I press trembling fingers to his cheek. He grasps my hand, lays it beside me.

"I'm going to get you some help," he says as he rises, leaves me alone once more, bereft of his comforting presence.

"Eric," I call out.

No response.

Quiet words squirm through an open doorway, climb up the side of the bed upon which I lie, squat upon my chest, their baleful gaze thick with betrayal.

A man's quiet voice. "I'm not sure. No, the blood isn't hers. At least I don't think it is. But she's covered in it. No, I don't know her name. I saw her in the park this morning, looking like she was in some serious trouble. I offered my help, but she took off. Yes, and now she's back. Please send someone as fast as you can."

Silence. The soft rustle of shoes over carpeting.

Why Eric? Why have you abandoned me again? Why have you betrayed me to Mother Gothel?

The voices inside begin to mutter and mumble. They prowl the lightless depths of my mind, poke my sluggish thoughts into wakefulness.

A name spoken.

Rapunzel!

Repeated.

Rapunzel!

A face peeks around the corner, eyes shadowed and dark.

Venom ignites caustic flames. They wriggle and writhe, scalding bone, stripping serenity.

Let down your hair!

Miserable rapture.

Then I may claim your golden stair!

I scream.

The outline of a tall, lanky figure fills the doorway, blotting out the light spilling into the room.

I lurch from the bed, the center of a thrashing and flailing maelstrom.

He drops his phone, staggers from the doorway, shielding his face and body as my hair throws him across the room.

Confessional

Detective Locke

Late afternoon shadows stretch over the open doors of Our Blessed Mother parish, crawl to the base of the gray marble font filled with holy water in the nave. Warm air from the outside shivers in the dimmer artificial light, brushes the water's surface.

Locke hovers at the edge of the bombed-out devastation littering the rear of the church. Split and splintered wood lies scattered across the tiled floor, moldering beneath the artificial fluorescent light raining down from the ceiling. The smell of death lingers, clinging to the broiling air, refusing to release its grip. He scans the debris, mind churning, gut knotting.

Two parish priests gruesomely murdered in less than twenty-four hours. In their parishes. Both wrapped in winding tangles of thick red gold hair that seems to have pierced their bodies like spear tips and, in this case, dismembered the victim.

Crime scene technicians wander ant-like through the mangled chaos, marking potential evidence, snapping photographs, bagging debris and wreckage. Scattered about the sea of destruction lie the limbs and parts of what used to be a person clothed in the remains of a priest's frock and entangled in ropy strands of crimson-smeared red gold hair.

Locke kneels near the decapitated torso, examines the remnants of the maimed and ruined violet and blue-tinged petals of a flower shoved into the collar similar to the bellflower, aka Rapunzel, according to his crime scene technician, found on the body of Augustus Matthews. He opens his notebook, writes a few lines, opens his phone, shuffles through a few photos until he finds what he is looking for. He holds the photo near the flowers jutting from the body, frowning. They are the same.

He carefully peels back the shredded remains of the shirt. The same symbol carved in Father Matthews's chest is carved in the chest of this body as well.

Quiet footsteps cause him to look over his shoulder. "Are these the same flowers we saw at the first crime scene?"

The technician stares for a moment, nods. "Bellflowers," he says. "But I can't confirm if they are from the same bunch without testing them."

"Can you have your grandmother look at them?" Locke asks.

"She passed five years ago. Cancer."

"Sorry for your loss."

The technician shrugs. "It is what it is. I'll send some samples to the CBI lab in Denver, see if they can do a genetic comparison."

"In the meantime, find out if there are any florists or gardening centers in the Fort Collins area that grow and sell bellflowers." Locke examines the red gold strands wrapping the body, the way they twist and turn into long, sinuous braids that crawl across the bloody clothing, piercing flesh, sprouting outward into winding and spiraling vine-like shoots, tendrils, and runners. He studies the bellflower stalk jutting from the shirt collar.

Also known as Rapunzel.

Locke crushes a surprised chuckle. Rapunzel? As in the Brothers Grimm fairy tale of the same name? He shakes his head. It can't be that simple, can it? Rapunzel wasn't a spree killer that used her impossibly long hair to murder priests. But she was banished to the wastelands by her caretaker, Mother Gothel, after getting pregnant with twins.

Memory twists his thoughts. Mother Gothel. He interviewed a Mother Gothel. Ten years ago during his investigation of the murders of Annabelle and Howard Grimm. Their granddaughter, Rosalinde, missing for three years after the murders, had been their prime suspect, but she'd never been brought to trial. Instead, she'd been committed to Sacred Heart Psychiatric Hospital after her mind completely unscrewed itself from reality. Rosalinde had accused a Mother Gothel of murdering Eric Homestead, another missing teen from the area, and stealing Rosalinde's twin daughters from her womb.

"Locke?" Keith Fox, his face pale and a little green.

"Yeah."

"Our witness is ready if you are."

He follows Fox from the back of the auditorium. "Tell me about our witness," he says.

Fox pauses, searches the pages of his notebook. "Two young girls. Twins. Ten. With their grandmother. Came to see the priest. Won't say why. They walked in at the end of the—"

"You got names?"

"Uh—"

Locke opens the door to an office in the back of the parish, stares into tense, cold, and calculating eyes the color of burnished platinum belonging to an elderly woman dressed in a flowing black high-collared and long-sleeve dress. She stands beside the two young girls. Twins. Seated beside each other in plain, wooden office chairs. A wrinkled, paper-thin hand drapes over each girl's shoulder.

Shivers shimmy down Locke's spine. He clears his throat.

"Miriam Gothel. Abigail and Anna," Fox says.

"Mother Gothel," Locke says, the name clipped and tense.

Miriam Gothel offers a cold and unfriendly smile that stretches her slender lips across caffeine-stained teeth. "Detective Locke. A pleasure to see you again after all these years, considering the grim circumstances. But, if you recall, I prefer Sister Miriam."

"These are your granddaughters?" Locke asks. "I thought nuns weren't allowed to—"

"I am their guardian," Sister Miriam says. "They are my wards and residents of our children's home." Steel courses through her expression. "I'm afraid the other detective made an assumption based on a lack of factual information."

"And your names are?" Locke gazes at each girl in turn, a queasy feeling slithering through his stomach. The girls are vaguely familiar, but he can't grasp the elusive memory hovering just beyond his reach.

"My name is Anna," the girl on Locke's left says in a quiet voice.

He smiles, gazes at her twin on his right. "And you are?"

"Her name is Abigail," Anna says.

"Be quiet!" Abigail hisses. "He's not our friend. He smells like—"

"Girls, please." Sister Miriam squeezes their shoulders. They wince. Abigail pinches her lips closed, violent emotions rumbling behind her eyes. Anna looks down, chagrin squatting across her slender face.

"Before you ask any of your ridiculous and annoying questions, Detective, we don't know who murdered Father Oldham. And if you don't mind, I would like to take the girls home. They've been through quite an ordeal today and need familiar surroundings to help them calm down. You may forward any questions you have for us through our attorney." She hands Locke a card, draws Anna and Abigail to their feet.

Locke lifts a brow. "Maybe I should be treating you as a person of interest in this murder, rather than witnesses," he says.

Abigail glowers. "I told you he wasn't our friend."

Anna's face pales. "Father Oldham was our friend, but we didn't—"

"Then tell me what you saw," Locke says. "I was told you saw the attacker's face. Was it a man or a woman?"

"Detective."

The warning seething through Sister Miriam's tone scrapes Locke's mind. He brushes it aside. "Give me something."

Sister Miriam squeezes Anna's shoulder. Shakes her head.

"A woman," Anna blurts, ignoring Sister Miriam's warning. "And she looked like me and Abigail. Only older."

"Enough!" Sister Miriam yanks the girls from their chairs and shoves them through the office doorway. She turns and glares at Locke. "As I have said," she says, "any questions for myself or the girls are to go through our attorney."

Before he can respond, Sister Miriam slips through the door, propelling Anna and Abigail before her.

Locke stands and stares, his mind grappling with Anna's last comment about their killer. *She looks like me. Only older.* He thinks of Rosalinde Grimm ten years ago. An incomplete and fractured image forms. He shakes his head. Not possible. Rosalinde Grimm is locked up behind the padded walls of Sacred Heart Psychiatric Hospital.

Centerfold

Twilight hovers across a bruised and battered sky. Fire red stains the western horizon, flashing flames across the emptiness glaring down on the retreating daylight, night snapping at its heels like a famished wolf. The jagged outline of quiet, darkened buildings marches down the road. Streetlamps burn with yellow-white light, their creamy radiance chasing back the deepening dark from the sidewalks.

An unpretentious cathedral stands off from the row of buildings lining either side of the empty street. It sits in the center of a square parcel, dotted with maples and blue spruce. To the side slumbers a playground, its occupants waiting patiently for the morning light and the herd of children that will graze upon its delicacies.

A warm wind stutters through the air, chafing my scalp. Stubble dots the scarred landscape, forming an itching field of mown hay. I rub it, wincing as it pricks my fingertips, before settling my hat down over the dead field.

The floral chiffon dress I wore for Father Confessor Augustus Matthews sags over my body, the white fabric smeared with blood, clotted with goo, and torn and tattered. I did not mean to fall apart, but the weight of my own damnation grows too heavy for me to carry. Even now, I feel my soul vanishing, sucked dry by the demons squirming through my body, my mind.

Mother Yasmina warned me, tried to dissuade me from my course of vengeance. I refused to listen, driven by my need and my desire. Eric, my beloved, stolen from me. My unborn children ripped from my womb by Mother Gothel as an eternal penance for my sin. My freedom and sanity taken.

Ten years of my life gone.

Revenge is the ultimate drug, the only one I cannot free myself from. An eternal addiction.

And though my Oma and Grandpapa tried to protect me from our curse by forcing me to keep my hair shorn throughout my childhood, my restless soul refused to remain quiet. Hence, Grandpapa's insistence that I accept Mother Gothel's invitation of salvation and peace.

A false promise until she no longer needed my demon and could cast me aside as if I were nothing more than refuse. I had been meant for another, my children born from that unholy union meant as pawns in her maddened quest to purge our world of demonic possessions. But I had committed the ultimate sin and fallen in love with the boy meant to be my jailer. Together, we defied Mother Gothel and her scheme, believing that our love and determination could thwart her plans.

We were horribly wrong.

Eric, my beloved, murdered. My children stolen from me at their birth. My curse imprisoned but not expunged.

What Mother Gothel wanted with my tainted offspring, other than to punish me, I did not know. I did not care. I would have them back, removed from Mother Gothel's control, the Heralds of the Seventh Seal destroyed, and the architect of my lifetime of suffering dead.

My unanticipated altercation with my daughters at Our Blessed Mother parish unhinged another portion of my failing sanity. Abigail's ire unsettles me. Anna's inheritance of our curse disturbs me.

I do not have much more time to save them.

I stare at the sign, hunkered down into concrete and asphalt. Saint Anthony's Parish. My final thirst for vengeance before Mother Gothel. A third mortal sin. The fourth and final one saved for Mother Gothel.

Saint Anthony's Parish is an anachronism; its original iconic sixties-style architecture melding with twenty-first-century fashion. Steeped in historical tradition, yet oozing modern-day obnoxiousness, the church occupies an uncomfortable space between yesterday and today. The rectory cowers quietly amidst the clutter.

I wander through the grounds, a desert island in the center of a stormy sea, undiscovered and alone. The voices whisper to me, their quiet chatter almost soothing despite the message of murder dripping from their sibilant tongues. My scalp itches, but I ignore the desire to remove my hat and scratch the itch. I feel the edges of my putrefying soul nibbled away, chewed to the rotten, moldering core. I wonder at the rot, but the voices and the need for vengeance propel me forward.

I pause upon the stoop of the rectory. Pristine virginal light seeps past the edges of the curtained windows, chasing back the darkness. My hand rests upon the door latch. The demons chatter through my thoughts, eager for their next soul and the taste of corruption infusing a supposed man of God.

I remove my hat, crush it at my side, recite the rhyme that will release my curse and allow my hair, the instrument of my vengeance, to run wild through the approaching chaos.

I ring the bell.

The porch light flares to life.

The door opens.

The priest peers out from the illusory safety of the open doorway. He hesitates, a moment of concern evolving into leery watchfulness. "May I help you?"

"Father Isaac Deighton?" I ask.

"Yes?"

I smile, recite the final verse of my rhyme. Exquisite pain erupts from my shaved scalp. My hair leaps from my head, thrashes the air, the strands winding into braids that snake toward him.

His eyes widen. He stumbles back, hands flailing.

The ends of my hair whip the air, draw a bloody line down the top of his hand to his wrist. He cries out, snatches his hand back, protecting it within the confines of his robes.

I giggle, step into his front room, close the door behind me. "Sit," I command. While he watches my writhing hair, I place a miniature tape recorder on the lamp stand beside his chair.

"I thought you might like a short respite from corrupting souls." I smile, press play. "Centerfold" by the J. Geils Band plays. I dance, my body gyrating, my growing hair squirming and twisting as I prance around his chair.

He stares, mouth hanging open, shock pouring from his eyes. At the first chorus, he stands. My hair catches him, shoves him back into his chair. The song continues, my body bumping and grinding, my hair whirling and twirling, its length growing, the strands thickening.

Sweat trickles down the sides of my face, soaks my shoulders, strays to the neckline of my grime-smeared dress.

The music continues. The energy intensifies. Lights shatter, spraying glass. The priest cries out, shields his face from the slivered shards raining down on him. Shadows leap from the corners. The voices jabber. Taloned fingers stretch out, tear and rip.

The priest screams.

The song ends.

My hair drives spiked ends at him as ecstasy clutches my heart and throttles my soul.

The screak of squirming hair tightening around wrists and ankles, binding limbs to the chair arms and legs.

A moan. Eyes fluttering open, widening with terror. Flickering light glinting off dazzling blue. How bright his eyes are, even now, in the uncertain light. The lean face and strong, narrow chin.

Tainted attraction tugging at my heart, pulling memories from the depths of regret and shattered dreams.

He had pretended to befriend me in my earliest days as a ward of the Heralds. Our friendship flowered quickly, harvested love and passion.

My eyes stray to his lips, still delectable and oh so kissable. I remember those lips and their taste. His late-night visits to my tower chamber. His sweet words drizzling honey as he sought to take my body and my mind. The excitement and allure of forbidden fruit, plucked from the tree under the nose of the caretaker. Or so he had tried to convince me.

And I would have fallen but for the rumors whispered through the halls. Rumors of a fresh young maiden chosen by Mother Gothel to birth the children destined to be the tip of the Heralds' spear in their war against the Father of Lies.

Rage at the betrayal from the woman who professed to save me from demon possession and insanity. My consolation in the arms of Eric Homestead. Our burgeoning love. Truly Forbidden.

I gaze down upon a sculpted chest, swaths of curly, dark brown hair peeking hesitantly past lacerated and shredded black and white cloth. Blood soiling the ripped fabric.

A blood-smeared braided gag, torn from my whirling hair, pulling tight into the china-fine mouth, knotting around the back of his shorn head.

"Please." The word mumbled past the hair tangled gag grinding into the creases of his mouth.

The door in my heart cracking open to allow uncertainty to peek through.

Rage stomping it into an oozy mush.

Smiling at him, I stroke his goose-down pillowed cheek, lean over to brush trembling lips over the velvety carpet.

"Too late," I whisper, nipping his ear playfully, standing to regard him critically. "Too late."

A spasm ripples through my skull, stinging my mind with a stampede of pins and needles. Razor-edged gossamer tickles my neck and shoulders, skims down my chest, meandering over my arms.

I close my eyes and shudder, biting my bottom lip with intensifying fervor.

When I open them, he stares, terror running from his eyes down his cheeks, dripping from his trembling chin. The collar of his shirt glistens with it.

Grinning, I straddle his lap, brace his head between my hands, lick the horror from his face. He shudders.

"Do you remember me?"

He nods.

My smile deepens. "I'm glad. You pretended to be my first love in a place where real love was forbidden, unless sanctioned by the witch. Do you recall our time together?"

His Adam's apple slides up and down. His gaze glistens with terrified tears. Sweat beads upon his brow. He blinks it from his eyes, tries to speak around the knotted plaits entwining his mouth, the words mumbled and mostly incoherent, but I understand enough.

He utters a falsehood. A bribe.

I squeal with delight at his feeble attempt to deceive me still. I touch my chest in mock flattery. "I am honored that you continue to profess your undying love for me," I say. "Truly." The smile I wear fades, devolves into a scowl. My hair thrashes into the air, the needle-tipped ends stinging the flesh beneath his shredded frock. "But I think you continue to confuse duty and love, even now." I lean closer, touch lips to his ear. "Would you not agree?"

Hesitancy, born of indecision.

I watch and wait, though the demons inhabiting me continue to grow more restless. They hunger for their promised meal and will not be put off much longer.

He finally jerks a nod.

I grin down at him, feigning delight at his too late forced honesty.

"One question I have for you," I say. "Answer it truthfully and I may yet allow you to live, though perhaps not as comely as you are now."

His eyes widen.

I touch my nose to his, gaze into his eyes. "Where are my daughters?"

He trembles. His head shakes, the words I do not want to hear slipping out from between the winding strands slowly strangling his mouth. I know what his answer must be. My daughters are hail and whole and under the thrall of Mother Gothel. I also suspect where she must hide them, where she hid all of us from an unsuspecting and uncaring world. But I still need to hear the words from him before I tear his body and rip his soul from his tattered and torn spirit.

"She has them." He gags, head snapping forward and back on his clenching neck.

Disillusionment wrenches my heart.

He opens his mouth, but there are no words, only ragged retching and a coarse mewling.

I shush him, slide the backs of my fingers down his cheek, brush his forehead with my lips, and stand.

"I confess," I say. "I did not think you would answer truthfully, even if you could. Of all the Fathers I have taken this day, I am almost sorry for the hellacious fate that awaits you."

Glistening golden strands writhe and waiver over his head.

Agony flames and burns my thoughts to ash, pulling euphoria and exhilaration behind its throbbing wake. My body spasms and contracts, arching my back.

I scream into the undulating shadow.

Oceans of swirling thickening strands of hair boil downward, slashing and stabbing and strangling, muffling his piercing howls.

The demons squeal their delight.

Shadows twitch and twist as I stagger through the front doorway, a set of car keys strangled in my quivering hand, the golden metal smeared with a gooey crimson. A murky night hovers in the blackened sky. Behind the stale, musty mist, the stars are dimmed like tarnished silver.

My knotted, mangled tresses trail behind me, rasping and hissing as they scratch drunken paths across grimed wood and fouled carpet, returning to their home in my skull.

I pause at the threshold, gasping for breath, cringing from the throbbing agony that grinds my mind into a sodden mush. An owl hoots from a nearby tree, its eerie call slinking through the shuddering air before it vanishes into the mildewed, cloudy blanket of the night.

I shove myself from the doorway, lurch through uneven, tenderly tended flower gardens beside the rectory, the last of my tangled braids slithering from the gaping darkness into my pounding skull. I drag the keys against the siding, the rasping sound jabbing needles through my thoughts as I stumble into the side door of a small, silent garage hunching near the side of the rectory.

The door opens on screeching hinges.

Inside is the priest's car.

The Brothers Grimm

DETECTIVE LOCKE

Clear Butte Community Church. The home of Pastor Thomas Eldridge.

Locke's pen scratches the words across the page. A haunting silence envelops him despite the stormy turmoil surrounding him, quiet voices, the rapid-fire click of digital cameras, and the hushed scuff of cleanroom booties across the wooden floor. He lifts the pen from the page, studies the scene.

Furniture wreckage scattered across the room. The jumbled remains of a small dining room table driven into a corner. A shattered window, glass shards strewn across the small garden bordering this side of the house. Gaping holes in the ceiling, jagged ends dripping paint flakes, smashed wood, and drywall dust. Broken and fractured table lamps thrust into walls, their debris pressed into the crevices between floor and walls. The odor of sweat-laden fear stalking the air, mixed with blood and death.

Locke stands in the center of the chaos. His pen tip returns to the page, writing more notes, drawing diagrams of the disorder surrounding him. Tufts of red gold hair peek from the ragged margins of the holes gawking from above, clutch the serrated edges of broken glass. He kneels down, pokes a clump of hair the same color and consistency discovered at his two previous crime scenes. His thoughts turn tornado-like through his mind, casting a grotesque image on the screen of his childhood memories...and his more recent cases.

Fairy tales, folktales, and folklore. Stories of magic and monsters recorded and told by the Brothers Grimm. One story in particular that haunts his reminiscences.

Rapunzel. The story Olivia had been obsessed with. The infant daughter traded by her father to a witch for a nightly supply of rampion from her garden on the other side of a wall. Also known as rampion bellflower, bellflower, or Rapunzel, picked by the man to satisfy his pregnant wife's craving for rampion salad. The rhyme spoken by the witch and the prince to tell the girl trapped in an impenetrable tower to lower her hair to be used as a climbing rope. Rapunzel's pregnancy, the witch's rage, and perceived betrayal. The prince thrown from the tower window. Rapunzel exiled to a desolate wasteland where she gives birth to her twins. But a happy ending when Rapunzel and her prince are reunited to live happily ever after.

Only, in this story, Rapunzel seemed to be the avenger. And happily ever after wasn't her goal.

Or was it?

A chill crawls through his skull. Locke shakes his head and stands. He surveys the scene again. Eyes avert as his gaze touches theirs. The muffled buzz of faint conversation stutters and dies. He knows what they call him. The growing list of nicknames and monikers traded through the department because of his personal history and the cases he works. Weird and bizarre. The creepy, freaky, and crazy. The stuff that defies logical explanation.

He grimaces, nods to a nearby technician. "Make sure you bag and tag everything."

The crime scene technician pauses, his gaze focused on the smashed window and the glass splinters, the clumps of hair caught on the glistening glass knife blades. He nods, marks the location, snaps several photographs before resuming his crime scene road trip.

Locke turns the other clues over in his mind. The stems of bell-flower left behind on the two victims they have so far. What is the significance? And the emblem carved into the two priest's chests. Religious somehow? He's not familiar with the sigil and nothing has popped from their files yet, either. But the two are connected. Some-how.

For a moment, Locke imagines the girl from the folktale alive and rampaging through Clear Butte, using her flowing locks to murder priests. But why priests? One Catholic, the other Protestant. What is the connection? The brief description of their assailant from their only witness lies flat and lifeless in his thoughts. *She looks like me, but older.*

Anna and Abigail, two sides of the same coin, wearing the same face as his spree killer. *She looks like me, but older.* He's missing something important, but he doesn't know what he doesn't know, and he can't remember what he can't remember.

Which brings him back to Mother Gothel and her home for or-phaned and unwanted children. Her defiance and secrecy. The same calculated unresponsiveness he encountered ten years ago when he confronted her about Eric Homestead and Rosalinde Grimm, who accused Gothel of murdering Eric and stealing her twin daughters. *She looks like me, but older.* Abigail and Anna were about ten, weren't they? The right age. And twins.

Ten years ago, Gothel accused him of fishing. Irritating, but she wasn't wrong. This time, she slams the door in his face with her attorney. He pulls the card she gave him from his notebook. Her attorney's name is blazoned across the cloth-like white surface, trailed by a number of abbreviations.

Locke snorts. Despite his somber mood, a smile twitches the corner of his mouth.

"Locke?" Keith Fox.

"Yeah." He shoves the card back into the pocket of his notebook.

"You good?" Keith's tone dripping with worry.

He nods. "Running some things through the grist mill."

A hard stare cast on flint. "You seem a little...distracted."

"I'm good. What've you got?"

"Your witness or victim. Take your pick. In the back. He's ready if you are."

"Right." Locke wanders in the indicated direction, noticing the additional holes punched through the walls, smashed picture frames hanging disheveled and crooked from their hangers.

He finds the man sitting on a bed, face bruised and battered, jaw beginning to swell, one eye blackened, the other roving aimlessly through the emptiness. His hands shake in his lap, worrying themselves into knotted fists that untangle almost as quickly.

"Thomas Eldridge?"

The man looks up, takes a moment to register Locke. He nods.

Locke, his lips pursed, looks at the paramedic. The man shrugs.

"He needs some stitches above his left eye. His nose is broken, and he definitely has a couple of broken ribs. But he refuses transport. Nothing more I can do from here."

"Thanks."

"Mr. Eldridge, I'm Detective Locke. Are you sure you don't want to go to the hospital and get checked out more thoroughly? Maybe get your ribs wrapped up, have that eye stitched up and your nose set?"

Eldridge looks at him, pinches his nose between his hands, takes a deep breath, wrenches it back in place.

Locke winces.

The paramedic grunts, jerking the hint of a smile. "Guess we don't need to worry about the broken nose."

"Do you mind if I sit?"

Eldridge shakes his head.

Locke takes possession of the small rocker-recliner in the corner, nods toward the paramedic.

"I'll hang out in the front room for a few more minutes in case he changes his mind."

Locke watches him leave, turns to Eldridge. "Mr. Eldridge—"

"Tom."

"Tom," Locke says. "I appreciate your time, but we can continue this at the hospital if you're not up to it right now."

Eldridge sucks in a trembling breath, presses his hands down on his lap, fingers spread. They shake.

Locke notices the cuts and scrapes crisscrossing his arms, the crusted blood matting his hair. "What's your affiliation with the Clear Butte Community Church?"

"I'm the pastor," he says. "We're a nondenominational group."

"And you live here?"

Eldridge nods. "The house is part of the grounds, one of my benefits."

"And your family?"

"Single," Eldridge says. "Never married. No children."

Unusual. But what does he know? Olivia had been the religious one in their family. Until she wasn't. Locke ponders his next question. "Any family we can contact for you? Parents? A sibling? Friends? Someone you can stay with for a few days while we sort through the mess?"

"I...I can't stay here?"

"Don't know how long it will take us to release the scene. In the meantime, you need to be with someone."

"Right. I...uh. I can call someone in the congregation, I guess."

"Sure." Locke consults his notes. "So, tell me what happened."

Eldridge snorts a jittery laugh. "You won't believe me," he says. "I don't believe it myself."

"Try me."

A quiet, hysterical giggle. Eldridge sucks in a breath. "Her hair," he begins, stops, clenches his fists in his lap, squeezing the knuckles white. He looks at Locke, dread gleaming from his eyes. "Her hair...it was alive."

Locke shivers. "Alive?"

"Yeah. Alive. Crazy, right?" Eldridge closes his mouth, opens it, runs his hand through his hair. He shakes, his complexion blanching, eyes round and glassy.

Locke reaches over, touches his leg. "Take your time," he says. "Do you need a glass of water?"

Eldridge shakes his head. "I was on the phone talking to nine-one-one—"

"Why?"

"I thought she was in trouble. She looked like she was in some kind of trouble. Covered in blood, her dress torn. But she didn't have any hair when I first saw her. Her scalp was...barren."

"Bald?"

"No, barren, like a field that's been razed."

"Did she come to you for help?"

"I...she broke into my office. It's at the back of the house. I thought the blood was hers. I cleaned some of it off, but I didn't see any wounds or injuries. That's when I called nine-one-one. I didn't understand why someone could be covered in so much blood, not their own."

One of Olivia's demons peeks out from behind tattered memories. Locke shoves it back down, stomps it into the mud and the mire. "Go on."

"She must have heard me on the phone. I heard a scream. And then she blew through the bedroom door like a hurricane, wreathed in a tornado of hair. Her hair attacked me, beat the crap out of me, threw me into the wall. And then she was gone."

Locke stares, searching for the lie, the subterfuge, wondering if this pastor has been engaging in another sort of behavior. "I have to ask," he says. "Are you taking any medications or other...drugs that might make you hallucinate?"

"No."

Nothing more.

"Is this woman a member of your congregation?"

"No. I've never seen her before this morning."

"This morning?"

Eldridge nods. "In the park across the street, just after dawn. I was on my morning run when I saw her sitting on a bench. She wore the same dress, and there was a white high-heeled shoe on the bench beside her. Both were bloody, but not as bloody as she was this time." He touches the top of his head. "She wore a hat, like a sunhat...something like that. When I asked her if she needed help, she took off."

"And you'd never seen her before?"

Another shake of his head.

Locke writes in his notebook, jots a few thoughts in the margins, draws arrows to connect his meandering dots. He turns back to his notes from Saint Thomas Aquinas parish, his attention drawn to his descriptions of the crime scene and the name of the priest. "Did you know a Father Augustus Matthews, the parish priest at Saint Thomas Aquinas parish?"

Eldridge looks up. "*Did* I know?"

Tread carefully. Locke remains silent, waiting.

Eldridge nods. "Yeah," he eventually says. "We served on the same interdenominational committee for Clear Butte."

More notes scribbled in the margins. Locke flips back to his notes from Our Blessed Mother church. "And what about Father Sebastian Oldham, the parish priest at Our Blessed Mother parish?"

"What's going on?"

"Answer the question. Please."

Hesitance. Uncertainty wandering across Eldridge's face. He nods eventually, looks down at his shaking hands.

"From the same interdenominational committee?

Another nod. "We also played chess together...occasionally."

Locke notices the pause before Eldridge says, 'occasionally.' Suspicion pricks the hairs along the back of his neck. "Do you recognize this emblem?" He holds up a computer-generated image of the sigil carved into the chests of Matthews and Oldham.

Eldridge stares for a heartbeat, looks away, shakes his head, mutters, "No."

Another tell. Suspicion blooms, pushes its intoxicating stalk through the soil, where it flowers.

"Are you familiar with bellflower?" Locke asks.

A flinch. The tightening of muscles. The clenching of the jaw. It's all Locke can do not to scream at Eldridge to confess. But to what, exactly?

"Bell what?"

"Bellflower," Locke says. "It's also called Rapunzel."

Eldridge shakes his head, his reaction too swift, the denial too forceful. "No," he says. "Never heard of it."

"Can you describe the woman you spoke to in the park this morning and who attacked you tonight?"

"Locke."

He ignores his name, focuses on Eldridge, waiting and watching.

"Locke!"

"What?"

Keith Fox stands in the doorway, shaking, his face pale, eyes haunted. "We've got another one."

Flesh of My Flesh

I TURN OFF THE car headlights as I coast to a creeping stop behind a stand of pine trees bordering the Mission of Hope Home for Wayward and Unwanted Children, Mother Gothel's veiled sanctuary for the Heralds of the Seventh Seal. The engine sputters and dies. I remain in the car, hands clenching the steering wheel. Despite the late evening cool air, sweat glistens from my forehead, slides greasy fingers across my barren skull. The pine branches rustle in the restless wind, breathing dark secrets into the night. Wood creaks. An owl hoots. Dusty pebbles scratch across the driver's door and window.

I step into the shadows.

The cast-iron fence guarding this side of the property remains as I remember it, rusted and broken, a gap large enough to allow a willow-wisp slender girl to shimmy through.

A pale, waning half-moon glares down from the gauzy velvet sky, casting an uncertain light into the swaying trees. Brief, glowing glimpses touch the needle-carpeted ground, tentatively brushing the deeper nighttime darkness. My footsteps gently crunch dried needles and dead leaves as I trudge through the brush toward the home.

My prison has not changed.

Bright virgin light bleeds from the landing, throwing back the deepening gloom. Softer yellowish light seeps through hazy grayish-white curtains along the third and fourth floor windows, casting hueless halos around the window frames, scrubbing dirt and grime from the dingy stone walls.

I let myself into the world of my nightmares through a pair of unlocked cellar doors.

Time slides past. It pauses at the end of a long, deserted hallway, stares back, waiting. My fragmented mind stands close to the abyss, its toes hanging over the ledge, suspended in the night. Below it, at the edge of oblivion, eyes peer upward into my thoughts. They glow with death, a ravening hunger dripping from crimson-stained teeth, dribbling over crooked and blistered lips.

Silence stands behind me, its soft breath brushing the back of my neck. My skin tingles where it caresses me, the shivers crawling with a million miniature fingers up and down my spine. Darkness crouches beside me, cloaking the long narrow hallway in a sullen, murky fog. The air shivers with anticipation, eager for the end of my journey.

I step into my extinction.

My bare feet quietly slap the black-and-white marble tiles, their chill touch sucking the warmth from my flesh. I run a lazy hand along one wall, fingers tracing the uneven trails meandering over rough, uneven plaster. A wooden splinter poking out from the cracked chair rail slices my fingertip. The pain stings. Blood oozes, its wet heat staining the wall.

Memories of Eric prance behind my eyes, obscuring my present and the reality of my situation. This is my end. Ten years of torment. One final death, and then I can reclaim what was ripped from my grasp, perhaps find peace as well.

A door creaks open, spilling garish lamp light into the maw of the dreary night in which I hide. A Father steps from Mother Gothel's office into the hallway, pauses and turns back. An old woman's voice slithers into the gloom, wraps constricting coils about his head. He shudders and nods.

I press against the wall, melding with the plaster, wood, and stone, their prickly fingers poking through the shredded fabric of my dress. A name hisses through my thoughts.

Rapunzel!

I quiver, clamp down on the voices beginning to stir from the depths of my doom. I cannot release the demons yet. I am too far from my final prize. If she knew I was here, that I was coming for her, she would have time to prepare.

And so, I wait. The voices grow restless, demanding that I release them. I refuse. They scowl and rage, pound the barriers I have erected. My scalp itches and stings with restless anticipation. A talon scrapes a gash across the remnants of my corrupted soul. I bite back the scream, digging my fingertips into the wall, allowing the sudden rending pain to reinforce my resolve.

The voices batter against my walls one last time, slink back into the darkness, sullen and pouting, their thirst far from slaked.

I draw in a quivering breath.

The door closes. The Father scurries down the hall, rounds a far corner, and is gone.

Relief?

No. Relief is too dangerous for me to feel.

Relief will come when my task is complete.

I pause at the closed door, place my ear to the rough-sanded oak planks, hear only solitude.

Another name spoken.

Rapunzel!

The demons stir once more, ravenous and restless. They crouch at the doorway of my mind, taloned fingers scratching at the disintegrating iron of my determination. Gnawing pain slices rivers through my thoughts. Blessed agony.

My hand reaches for the latch.

Let down your hair!

Light pours out in a flood, washing over me, pushing back the inky blackness clinging to my shoulders. For a breath, I almost feel unsullied, my soul clean like virgin snow.

The moment passes. The light of hope evaporates, leaving behind depravity and sin. My hair grows, stabbing its way through bone and flesh. It flails the air, twisting and twirling in a macabre dance.

I step over the threshold.

A fire burns in the hearth. Sparks spit from the fluttering flames and fall meteor-like to the flagstones hugging the base of the hearth. Tendrils of smoke wisp from under the mantel, melting into the ether. The floral scents of cedar and pine hover in the air. Lanterns glow from the walls, their lilting yellow-white light swaying to an unheard, secret music.

Mother Gothel sits behind an ancient oak desk, the burnished surfaces dulled by time and memory. She looks up as I slide into her chamber.

I expect surprise, fear. I am greeted by neither.

She smiles, but there is no friendliness in her expression as she pushes herself from the desk and stands, clasping her hands at her waist. It seems a lifetime since I saw her and my daughters at Our Blessed Mother parish. She glides around the desk, stands before it, vulnerable to my vengeance and my curse.

I stagger forward. My braids squirm and thrash, flail, twist and turn, forming a golden red halo around my head.

"Rosalinde," she says, her voice quivering slightly, fingernails drawn down a chalkboard. "I have been waiting for you." Another inhospitable smile, drooling malice.

I open my mouth to complete the rhyme.

Movement beside the fire snatches my attention.

My twin girls. Anna and Abigail. Ten years old. Emerald green eyes. Golden red hair that glistens in the frolicking firelight. Eric's mouth and slender chin. My swan-like neck, narrow shoulders and slim body. Fear glimmers from the eyes of Anna, malice gleams from the eyes of Abigail. The girl who challenged me this afternoon.

They look toward Mother Gothel, questions dripping from their lips.

The words hovering upon my parted mouth falter and fail, shattering into a million tiny pieces against the stone at my feet. My hair calms, retreats back into my skull, its final release unrealized, the malice driving it sinking into silence.

"May I present my daughters?" Mother Gothel gestures to each in turn. "Abigail and Anna."

She motions toward me. "Daughters of mine, this is Rosalinde, whom we saw this afternoon after she murdered our dear friend, Father Sebastian Oldham. As I told you, she is a former disciple, who came to us possessed by a demon. We tried to help her, but she defied our efforts and eventually succumbed to the demons' influence. She murdered another of our disciples, Eric Homestead, in a jealous rage and believes that I stole you from her at your birth." She pauses, glancing from Anna to Abigail. "She has come to kill us. What shall we do with her?"

I open my mouth, but the words will not form. The demons huddle within the detritus of my defeated vengeance, their unfulfilled purpose turning toward my defiled and rotting soul.

My strength flees. I fall to my knees, choking, the final words of my rhyme strangled. I reach out to my children, stolen from my womb by the witch standing before me, turned into her own instruments.

Anna continues to stare, confusion behind her eyes. She glances at my languishing hair, touches her shorn red gold locks. A question touches her lips.

Abigail, without hesitation, strides forward, brandishing a knife. Eric's knife. The same blade I stabbed Mother Gothel with during my escape ten years ago. She glares down at me but does not acknowledge the truth staring back at her from my tear-filled eyes.

Placing her fingers beneath my chin, she draws me to my feet. I am two heads taller than she, forcing her to look up at me. Our eyes mirrored reflections.

As I pull in an unsteady breath, she thrusts the knife into my chest. Pulls it out slowly, malice sparkling behind her eyes. A sinister smile stretches across her mouth. As I crumble, she catches me beneath my arms, brushes dispassionate lips across my cheek, allows my failing body to slip from her grasp and tumble to the floor.

Abigail drops the knife beside me, walks away.

Anna falls to her knees beside me. She sobs, her small, delicate hands pressing against the slashing hole gaping from my chest. "Someone help her, please," she says. "She is our mother."

Abigail strides forward, yanks Anna to her feet and drags her from me. Anna struggles, but Abigail's rage is too strong for her to resist, and she quickly falls quiescent.

A shadow rolls over me. The rustle of silken skirts scratches my ears. A calloused hand turns my head, forces me to stare up into my death. Mother Gothel stares down, mouth set in a tight line. She frowns as the door opens on well-oiled hinges, and nods.

"Make sure she is not found."

The voices whispering in my mind fall silent as the darkness claims me.

Oma

STRONG HANDS DRAG MY body from the trunk of a car, dump me on the hard, cold ground. Dirt puffs up, clogs my nostrils, and for a moment, I can no longer breathe as I am shoved by the toe of a work boot over the lip of a grassy hill. I roll down the uneven embankment, bang against rocks, tumble through brambles and scrub brush, settle at the edge of a meandering stream, my body splayed upon the muddy ground like a broken and stringless marionette.

Blood oozes from my chest with each struggling breath, sucking out the last of my strength. A diffident wind ruffles the grass, stroking my cheek, tugs at the loose ends of my tangled hair, the winding braids fraying and unweaving. The strands lay flat and limp in the grass and dirt, twitching and gasping.

The voices are quiet, blessedly. And yet, I miss their constant yammering; the eyes glaring with malevolence from the pitted depths of my moldering soul, their ravening hunger.

Is this how it ends?

Killed by my own flesh? My vengeance incomplete?

My vision tunnels. My thoughts scramble, begin to drop off the edge into the precipice.

Mein Liebling?

My head jerks up. "Oma?"

I am here, my love.

I reach up, fingers clawing frost-nipped air, the scrape of a dead hand. I sigh, allow my hand to drop to the ground. "I am undone by my own flesh."

Abigail is no longer of your flesh. But there still may be hope for the other.

Another knife twisting through my chest, piercing my heart.

To save the one, you must slay the other.

"I cannot."

You must.

"I will not."

You must!

Lightning cracks the night.

"I will not!"

I sit up, gasping, my heart racing. Agony lances through my chest. My hair dances in the night air. The demons jabber. Ghostly and corrupted fingers probe the inside of my wounded and torn flesh. Strands of my hair wind together and fountain from my skull into the hole gaping from my chest. I howl in agony.

The stars glare down from emptiness, beckoning.

I climb the embankment, stumbling into the Stygian gloom.

The Father leans against the side of his car, smoking a cigarette. His hands shake. Grayish smoke trails from his mouth into the night, vanishes before touching the waning moonlight. He turns, drops his cigarette, surprise skipping across his face.

My rhyme flows from my lips, wafts into the air, pulling my flailing and writhing hair with it.

He reaches for the pistol beneath his jacket, fumbles it as the spear-tipped ends of my hair drive through his body into the side of the car. He slumps to the ground, dead eyes wide in shocked surprise, his mouth distorted into a gaping hole. I fish his car keys from his pocket, muscle his dead weight to the edge of the grassy knoll and push him over. His body tumbles down the embankment, disappears into the murky gloom.

Un-Locked

Detective Locke

Locke slumps in his chair, elbows propped on his desk, hands pressed into his forehead, papers and photos spread around him. He studies the chaos, asking, cajoling, begging for insight. But the papers and pictures remain tight-lipped and silent. He sighs in frustration, pushes himself away. His chair rolls across the tiled floor, plastic wheels rumbling over the linoleum, bumps into the coffee station, rattling ceramic coffee cups, and jarring the coffee maker.

He sighs and closes his eyes, rubs the grit from them.

The police station is empty and quiet except for the electric hum of the HVAC and the calm whoosh of artificially cooled air. He looks at his desk; the disorder spread across the surface.

What is he missing?

Why can't he connect the dots?

Because the only thing connecting those dots and his spree killer were three dead priests, Rapunzel left on each dead body, a mysterious symbol carved into the chests of the three victims, and two witnesses who told the same impossible story. An insane and horrific version of Rapunzel.

William?

Locke finches.

"Please. Not now."

William? Why won't you talk to me?

"Because you're dead."

I never stopped loving you.

He grinds his fists into his eyes. "I can't."

The sound of water rushing from a faucet, splattering onto the tiled floor, covering the bathroom floor in a sea of red-tinged water. Olivia leaning against the wall, dead eyes staring, blood leaking from the hole in her head, dribbling down her shaved skull.

His horror and desperate need to find another reason for the deaths of his children and wife. How could he not have known Olivia was suffering—or at least suspected it?

I forgive you.

"For what?"

For not believing me. For not saving us.

Another image flashes of his wife and her shaved head.

Her shaved head. The book of *The Original Folk and Fairy Tales of the Brothers Grimm* on their bed, open to the story of Rapunzel. Olivia's journal. Her growing obsession with Rapunzel and her hair. Olivia's growing hatred and fear of her own hair.

Memories float to the surface.

Ten years ago, three months after the deaths of his wife and children. His first case after returning from his leave following the death of his family. A young woman in the Clear Butte Medical Center recovering from an attack. An abortion gone wrong or a brutal abduction of unborn children, something he'd never been able to determine. But the one thing that had struck him was that her head had been shaved. No, not just shaved, savaged.

Rosalinde Grimm.

She'd suffered a mental breakdown after learning that she was no longer pregnant and been committed to a psychiatric hospital.

Rosalinde claimed her children had been stolen from her womb by Mother Gothel, the owner and administrator of the Mission of Hope Home for Wayward and Unwanted Children. He'd interviewed Gothel, suspected that she was involved in the abduction of Rosalinde's children, as well as the murders of Eric Homestead and Rosalinde's grandparents. But there was no direct evidence, and he couldn't prove a connection between Mother Gothel and Rosalinde. The case went cold. And with Rosalinde committed, no reliable witness.

Locke springs from his chair, rips open his desk file drawer. The file from that case is the first in the drawer. His only unsolved case during his tenure with the Clear Butte PD, gone cold and silent as quickly as it had lit up his attention ten years ago. The one cold case that never truly let go of him, even after Rosalinde's commitment. He rifles through the contents until he finds a photo of Rosalinde. He ransacks the mess of documents littering his desk until he locates a hard copy of the sketch of their spree killer, places them side by side, compares them to the clandestine photos of Abigail and Anna he took earlier in the day.

His heart stutters.

Locke calls the psychiatric hospital where Rosalinde had been committed, is told that she and another patient, an elderly woman named Yasmina Bitterlich died after performing some kind of occult ceremony. Six months ago.

Another memory taps him on his shoulder.

Locke flips through his notebook.

The woman that had attacked Thomas Eldridge had called him Eric.

One last glance at the sketches of the woman with the cursed hair and Rosalinde Grimm.

Locke grabs his coat and runs from the station.

Let Down Your Hair

Rage propels me forward.

My beloved's brutal death.

The abduction of my twin daughters.

The utter loss of my family and any hope of happiness.

I drive the car of the Father I slaughtered in the woods through the gates barring the road leading to the Mission of Hope Home for Wayward and Unwanted Children. The car jerks as it collides with the wrought iron. The fencing tears from its hinges. Metal grinds and screams. The shattered gates clatter to the ground, skidding and bouncing off the hard-packed dirt.

Dust billows from behind the car as I race it down the meandering road, through the encroaching stands of pine and blue spruce, the moonlight cast into the blackness of nonexistence. The car emerges from the vacuum of nowhere minutes later. The dirt-smeared gray stone prison from my youth rears before me, monolithic towers scraping the night sky.

I push the gas pedal to the floor. The car lurches, skids and swerves through the lawn encircling the castle. I aim the car for the front doors.

The black, wrought iron and weather-worn oak doors explode inward, raining splintered wood and twisted metal into the immense and chasmal entrance hall. The giant, skeletal and spider-like chandelier hanging from the high arched ceiling torn from its moorings, crashes into the hood of the car, driving it down into the cracked and age-stained black-and-white checkered marble floor tiles.

My hair whips the air inside the car, smashes the windshield, blowing it from the frame. I crawl through the yawning hole and the debris littering the hood. I stride through the entry hall, thrashing and beating the stinging air.

Dust floats around me, clinging to my tattered dress, swirling around my hair, dancing to the silent music capering in my mind. The voices jibber-jabber, their eagerness driving me onward, my thoughts blazing with the fire of vengeance. My soul withers with each passing moment, blackened and rotted with depravity and evil.

A Father appears before me, blocks my advance. My hair crushes him in an instant. I move forward.

The sound of an approaching siren rings through the shattered doorway and into the hall.

I stand in front of the door leading to Mother Gothel's chambers.

I pause, my hair frothing the stale air into a frenzy.

Another Father approaches me, a cudgel in one hand, a knife in the other. I strike quickly, my hair shooting out like a flight of arrows. The ends run him through before he can take three strides toward me.

Mother Gothel stands beside her hearth. A fire burns inside the grate, the flames licking steaming oak, cedar, and pine. Steam boils, rises, and vanishes through the chimney. Sparks sputter, leaping to their deaths upon the flagstones stepping against the fireplace.

I do not see Anna or Abigail.

My heart sinks. Where are my daughters?

I step toward Mother Gothel. "Where are my children?"

She smiles and shakes her head. "You have no children here," she says. "I have, however, sent my daughters from this place to protect them from your delusional madness."

"You stole everything from me." I clench my fists and step forward. "Give me my daughters and I may still let you live."

A humorless chuckle. She unbuttons the top of her gown, pulls aside the seam. The scar of an old wound glowers from her wizened chest. "You attempted to end my life ten years ago, blaming me for your lover's suicide." She buttons her gown. "My dear, you were never pregnant. Everything you think you believe is not real, but rather a lie concocted by your ailing mind to ease the pain of your loss and suffering." She steps toward me, holding her hand out in contrition. "Allow me to help you this time."

A stampede of footsteps behind me.

A man with a gun. He aims it at me.

"Rosalinde Grimm?"

I stiffen, glance behind me. The face is familiar. From my past? I am uncertain.

Mother Gothel steps closer, holding her open hand toward me, beckoning me to accept her compassion and her help.

Fury burns beneath my skull, charring my thoughts to ash.

The voices chatter relentlessly inside my mind, licking the steam from my dying soul.

A gasp and uttered curses behind me.

My hair lashes the air, the ends snapping like a bullwhip.

"Rosalinde, please. Don't do what I think you're about to do." The man again. The sound of his voice shoves open a door I thought was closed and locked. A hospital room ten years ago. A police detective battering me with questions and accusations.

"She murdered my beloved," I say. "And she stole my children from me before they were born."

Mother Gothel shifts her gaze. "Detective Locke?"

"Please don't speak," he says.

"But you know what I say is the truth, do you not?" Mother Gothel gestures toward me. "She believes that she is Rapunzel from the story written by the Brothers Grimm. And she is possessed by demons. You've seen what she can do, what she has done? You are witness to her madness now. Need I say more?"

I tense. My hair flails and thrashes, growing, flowing and lengthening, the ends narrowing into razor-sharp needles, poised to strike.

Mother Gothel snorts. "Please remove her from my home, Detective. She is only dangerous to herself." She turns.

I attack.

My hair lashes out.

In that moment, Abigail materializes from the shadows cloaking the edges of Mother Gothel's study. She screams, launches herself, a knife clenched in her diminutive hand, coming between Mother Gothel and my hair. The ends strike, punching through her as if she were made of paper, stabbing through Mother Gothel and driving them together back into the wall.

A gunshot explodes.

"No!"

Anna's shrill voice?

Sudden stinging agony punches the side of my head. I spin, my feet tangling. I fall, my last vision, Mother Gothel and my sweet Abigail hanging together, limp from the wall.

Peace

I wake.

Subdued artificial light floats down from the tiled ceiling. Sterile air shivers through my hospital room. The odor of bleach and antiseptic spray floats on the back of the air, cleansing the empty spaces of disease and pestilence. An IV needle feeds fluid into my arm. Monitors beep with an inhuman rhythm, varied color lights skipping across the screen in harmony with the noises emanating from the machines.

My shaved head stings where the staples march across the scars crisscrossing my torn flesh. I gently rub my wounds with a trembling hand. My other hand lies at my side, manacled to the bed rail.

I stare into the shadows clinging to the far corners of my room, my thoughts a jumbled mass of tangles and knots. Images of my daughters parade across the landscape of my guilt. Abigail. Anna. Stolen from me before they were born. Raised by an evil, corrupt woman. Groomed for depravity and sin.

Abigail corrupted, beyond redemption by Mother Gothel. I could not save her.

Anna, perhaps lost to me as well. I do not know. But it does not matter. Both are gone, lost to me forever.

My beloved, dead, the victim of his own chivalrous heart.

A tear wells at the corner of my eye.

My breath hitches in my chest. Grief wanders the empty corridors of my broken heart. I listen for the voice of my Oma. But even she has abandoned me.

I am ready to accept the punishment I deserve.

Muffled voices outside my closed door. Silence.

It opens.

The detective who tried to help me ten years ago, who shot me this time, enters. Behind him, my ten-year-old face.

Anna.

The door closes behind them.

I tense. Waiting and uncertain. My lips tremble, the rhyme quivering at the tip of my tongue. But this time, nothing answers. I do not know whether to wail or cry.

The detective takes Anna's arm, leads her to my bedside, steps aside.

Anna grips the bed rail, her expression a chaotic mix of emotion. She stares into my eyes, evaluating, examining. Chewing her lower lip, she touches my arm.

"You are my true mother?"

I want to speak, but my voice has abandoned me. I nod. The tears well, slide down the sides of my face.

"I am your true daughter?"

Still, my voice does not appear. I nod again.

An instant of distrust. "Why did you abandon us to Mother Gothel?"

I open my mouth to speak. Incoherent noise dribbles out. I swallow. "You and your sister were stolen from me before you were born by Mother Gothel."

"Why would she do such a thing?"

"To punish me for falling in love and for defying her."

Anna nods, shifts her gaze to my shaved head. She rubs her clipped hair, then my wounded and damaged flesh with a shaking hand. "And your curse?"

I manage a shrug. "Your curse as well," I say. Guilt stabs me. "I am truly sorry."

Anna studies me. "Abigail chose her own path. One that I could not follow." She lifts her gaze to my barren scalp. "It is an evil thing. This curse of ours."

I nod. "But also a necessary thing. And part of our family heritage. It is something we shall carry throughout our lives. And when it is time, we shall pass it on to the next generation."

She seems to consider this. Her hand remains upon my scalp.

"Are you here to kill me?" I ask.

She smiles. "I had thought that perhaps I might." She shrugs. "But I would much rather be a true family."

Her other hand opens. In her palm is the key to unlock the handcuffs binding me to my hospital bed.

My gaze shifts to the detective.

His eyes drip an old, worn-out grief. "Take care of each other," he says. "It's something that was taken from me before I had the chance." He pauses at the door. "I think I'll take my officer to the cafeteria for a coffee and a donut. Goodbye, Rosalinde. I hope I never see you again."

Twisted Tales of Familiar Faces

If you enjoyed this bone-chilling retelling of the *Rapunzel* tale, don't miss out on the rest of this horrifying collection!

Humbug (Scrooge) - Andre Gonzalez

Sweethaven (Popeye) - RJ Clark

Timber Beast (Paul Bunyan) - A.K. Hughey

Alice (Alice in Wonderland) - Audrey Brice

Wish (Aladdin) - Courtney Konstantin

Quixote (Don Quixote) - Stephen Wertzbaugher

Arturius (King Arthur) - A.K. Hughey

Steamboat (Steamboat Willie) - Courtney Konstantin

Strangled (Rapunzel) - Stephen Wertzbaugher

Dethroning Oz (Wizard of Oz) - Audrey Brice

Scorned (Hercules) - Z.S. Diamanti

Check out the entire collection at www.m4lpublishing.com

Join our newsletter to stay up to date with all upcoming releases at www.m4lpublishing.com

Author's Note

This story would not have been written without the unwavering love and creative support of my wife, Kathy Wertzbaugher, to whom I owe a tremendous debt of gratitude. I would also like to thank my kids, Christine, Courtney, and Jeff, for their constant badgering, which kept me banging away at the keyboard, especially when the words didn't want to come.

A special thanks to my publisher, M4L Publishing, for their invitation to write for the Twisted Tales line, their belief in me during the dark times, and their support throughout the writing, editing, and publishing process.

Thanks to my editor, Nan Sampson Bach, who fearlessly goes where even angels fear to edit. Thanks to my writing coach, Audrey Hughey, for her continued support and tough love. And thanks to my Writing Mastermind Group, whose continuous words of encouragement and safe space allowed me to unburden my writer's soul without fear of judgment.

Enjoy this book?

We hope you enjoyed this release from M4L Publishing.

Reviews are the most helpful tools in getting new readers for any books. We don't have the financial backing of a New York publishing house and can't afford to blast our books on billboards or bus stops.

(Not yet!)

That said, your honest review can go a long way in helping us reach new readers. If you've enjoyed this book, we'd be forever grateful if you could spend a couple minutes leaving it a review (it can be as short as you like) on the site you purchased this book from.

Thank you so much!

About the author

Stephen Wertzbaugher has been fascinated with telling stories since the 3rd grade when he built a diorama and told the story of Doctor Doolittle to kindergarten classes. He wrote his first short story for an 8th grade English assignment about a coup of the US government using clones of key cabinet members. His true epiphany for spinning yarns came after seeing Star Wars in 1978 and remarking, "I want to tell stories like that."

A few decades later, he's living his dream, writing tales of horror, and urban and dark fantasy that allow him to chew on his worst fears.

www.ingramcontent.com/pod-product-compliance
Lightning Source LLC
Chambersburg PA
CBHW030900200726
48289CB00003B/839